The Gramma War

Kristin Butcher

ORCA BOOK PUBLISHERS

National Library of Canada Cataloguing in Publication Data
Butcher, Kristin, 1951–
The gramma war

ISBN 1-55143-183-1

I. Title.
PS8553.U6972G72 2001   jC813'.54   C2001-910017-5
PZ7.B9691Gr2001

First published in the United States, 2001

Library of Congress Catalog Card Number: 2001086173

Orca Book Publishers gratefully acknowledges the support of
our publishing programs provided by the following agencies:
the Department of Canadian Heritage, The Canada Council
for the Arts, and the British Columbia Arts Council.

Cover design by Christine Toller
Cover illustration by Krysten Brooker
Printed and bound in Canada

IN CANADA	IN THE UNITED STATES
Orca Book Publishers	Orca Book Publishers
1030 North Park Street	PO Box 468
Victoria, BC Canada	Custer, WA USA
V8T 1C6	98240-0468

03 02 01 • 5 4 3

For my parents,
who taught me that the impossible
just takes longer.

.... The second I walked into the bedroom, Claire started bossing me around.

"Touch my CDs and you're dead!"

Like I cared about her dumb CDs. Besides, I'd have to find them first, and that could take days. Claire's room was a disaster. There were clothes everywhere — mountains of them — heaped on her bed and dresser, oozing from drawers, and hanging in layers from the doorknobs.

Most of them were on the floor, though, and that made getting to the other side of the room a real challenge, especially since I couldn't see past the cardboard carton I was carrying. I tripped over something, and the box flew out of my arms onto the bed. I flopped down beside it.

How could Mom and Dad possibly think this was going to work?

Claire was a slob, and her room was a nightmare. Even clean — and I was pretty sure it never had been — it would've been creepy. The walls and ceiling were slathered with pictures of every actor and rock star Claire had ever drooled over during her entire fifteen years of life. I looked up. Above my bed was a glossy, life-size poster of some sweaty guy with a toothpaste-commercial smile, wearing nothing but ripped jeans. Every night before I closed my eyes, that was the last thing I'd see. If I didn't have nightmares, it would be a miracle.

I wondered if I could take down the pictures on my side of the room. Good idea. That way when Claire killed me, her wallpaper wouldn't get splattered with blood. I began feeling claustrophobic. My dresser and desk were jammed against the wall. Next to them, just far enough away to get the drawers open, was my bed. Actually, it wasn't even my own bed! I'd had to give that up too. For the next who-knew-how-long, I was going to be sleeping on the rollaway cot my parents kept for guests. Mom had aired the mattress, but it still smelled like the basement.

It'll just be for a little while. That's what my parents had said.

Who were they kidding? There was no telling how long I was going to be in this dungeon.

I unpacked the box and went back to my old room to pick up another load. My heart began to hurt as soon as I walked through the door. Maybe if I threw a fit, Mom and Dad would change their minds.

Not likely. The room was already starting to look like it belonged to someone else. The bed, with a boring beige spread now, had been moved away from the window. A new dresser stood where my old one had been, and my desk had been replaced with a chair, a small table, and a reading lamp.

I put the last of my stuffed animals into the box and took my Barkerville picture down from the wall. I blew the dust off the frame, polished the glass with my sleeve and stared for the ten thousandth time at the crowd of people in the photograph. Dressed in old-fashioned clothes, they were standing in front of a flimsy wooden building. The men were carrying pick axes and shovels, and some had coils of rope hooked over their shoulders. One was leading a pack mule, and another was running from the building, grinning and waving his arms in the air.

I'd snapped that photograph two years ago when my dad and I had gone to a reenactment of the 1860s gold rush in Barkerville. I'd never seen anything like it before — except in the movies. But these people weren't just acting. They were very serious, and everything was so authentic I had to keep reminding myself it wasn't real.

That was the day I'd started liking history. After that, every time there was a reenactment, Dad and I were there. It was great. I even began doing research ahead of time, so that I'd know what to expect.

Pretty soon I began wishing I was more than a spectator. So my dad suggested I join. But the lady in charge of History Repeats Itself — that was the name of the reenactment group — told me I was too young and said to come back when I turned twelve.

Now that was only two months away! I broke out in goose bumps just thinking about it.

I stuffed the photograph into the cardboard box and took a last look around the room. Reality set in again. I sighed and headed for the door. Then I heard a rustling noise.

"Oh, gosh!" I dropped to my knees beside the gerbil cage. "I'm sorry, guys. How could I forget *you?*"

Two velvet handfuls of fur scurried to the side of the cage and sniffed the air. I wiggled the tip of my finger through the bars, and the gerbils nibbled at it. Their little teeth tickled.

"It's moving day," I said. "Are you all packed?" As if they understood, they stopped chewing and stared at me with shiny black eyes. I let out a giant sigh. "Our new room is definitely not as nice as this one," I told them, "but I guess we'll survive. Mom says we're making a noble sacrifice and should be very proud."

But I knew better. This was no sacrifice. We'd been evicted! It was as simple as that. My grandmother was moving in and taking over my bedroom. And there wasn't a thing I could do about it.

It had all happened so fast. One day Gramma was in Winnipeg, where she'd lived for the last fifty years, and the next day her house had a *For Sale* sign in front of it, and she was on her way to Victoria.

My parents said it couldn't be helped. But I disagreed. Gramma had broken her hip. That's all. It would heal — just like when I'd broken my arm. So what if she couldn't do all the chores around her house any more? Uncle Mark and Aunt Meg could help out. They lived in Winnipeg too. They could cut her grass and shovel her snow. And they could drive her to her doctor's appointments and do her grocery shopping.

That's what I told my parents when they called a family meeting to explain what was going on.

But Dad shook his head. "There's too much to do," he said. "Your aunt and uncle travel a lot with their jobs. They wouldn't be able to stay on top of things."

"Couldn't Gramma hire someone to take care of her house and yard?" I asked.

"It would be very expensive, and there's no way of making sure Gramma doesn't get cheated."

"Why can't Gramma make sure?"

My parents had a private conversation with their eyes, and then my dad said, "Seniors can get forgetful, Annie, and sometimes people try to trick them. Gramma needs to be around people she can trust."

"Why can't she move in with Uncle Mark and Aunt Meg then?"

Claire rolled her eyes. "Good one, Annie. They could all share one big bed."

Mom gave Claire a dirty look.

"Well, excuse me for living!" Claire huffed. "But that *was* a pretty stupid question."

"No — it wasn't," Dad snapped. "We're trying to work through something important here, Claire. We could use *everyone's* cooperation."

Claire scowled but didn't say anything else. I wanted to cheer, but decided it probably wasn't a good idea.

"Unfortunately, that's not possible, Annie," Mom tried to explain. "Uncle Mark and Aunt Meg live in an apartment."

"It's got two bedrooms," I reminded her.

"Yes, but one is used as an office."

"It could be a guest room too," I pointed out.

"Gramma wouldn't want to live there, dear."

"Did you ask her?"

Again my parents exchanged *looks*. Then Dad completely ignored my suggestion and said, "I know this isn't an ideal solution — for anyone — but there really isn't any choice. Gramma is eighty-one years old. Her health has been deteriorating steadily for a while now, and this broken hip has really set her back. It isn't possible for her to live alone in that big house any more. He shook his head and frowned. "We knew it was only a matter of time until we had to do something. This accident just made us stop putting it off."

And so the decision had been made. Whether I liked it or not, my grandmother was coming to live with us. But I couldn't help wondering if she'd had any say in the matter.

.... When I came back with the last of my belongings, Claire was sitting on her unmade bed, clipping pictures for her wallpaper. Tangled in the rumpled sheets and magazine scraps, she looked like a large bird in a very untidy nest.

"Stop right there!" she said, wagging her scissors at my gerbils. "You are not bringing those smelly things into my room."

Instantly the hair on my neck stood up. Claire might be able to boss me around, but I wasn't going to let her insult my gerbils.

"First of all," I glared back at her, "Sandy and Sandy are not *things* – they're gerbils. Second of all, they don't smell. And third of all, this is not just *your* room any more."

Then I started walking again. But I couldn't have taken more than two steps before Claire jumped off the bed and blocked my way.

"I mean it, Annie. You're not keeping those horrible little rodents in here." Apparently she wasn't kidding around.

Well, neither was I. Through clenched teeth, I said, "They're not horrible, and yes, I am. Get out of my way."

I tried to push past, but Claire didn't budge. Suddenly I wanted to cry. This wasn't fair! I'd already lost my bedroom. Did I have to fight for my gerbils too?

"Look!" I yelled. "I have rights, you know!"

"Not here, you don't. This is my room, and what I say goes. So get those dirty things out of here."

That was the last straw. Now I was just plain mad.

"Dirty! Look who's talking. My gerbils are a million times cleaner than you are. Look at this place!"

Claire's eyes narrowed. "If you don't like it, you can get out too! I never wanted you here anyway."

"The feeling is mutual, I'm sure," I snarled back.

"All right, what's going on?" Mom was standing in the doorway, frowning. "I could hear the two of you all the way to the kitchen."

"It's Annie's fault."

"It is not! You started it!"

"You're the one who —"

"That's enough!" Mom raised her voice, and Claire and I both jumped. My mother hardly ever yells. Having caught our attention, she started talking normally again. "I shall ask one more time — what is going on? Claire, you first."

A hoity-toity, I-win-and-you-lose expression oozed across Claire's face. It was nauseating, and I wanted to throw up on her. She wrinkled her nose distastefully and pointed to my gerbils.

"Annie thinks she is going to keep *those* in here."

"And?" was all my mother said.

At that, Claire's mouth fell open. She looked at Mom as if she'd just beamed down from another planet.

"What do you mean *and*? And she's *not*!"

"So where do you suggest she keep them then?"

"I don't care where she keeps them! Just not here!"

"Don't shout, Claire. I am not hard of hearing." It was easy to tell Mom was losing her patience. "If you don't want the gerbils here, you had better have another location in mind."

"Why can't they stay where they were before?" Claire sounded defiant and desperate at the same time.

Mom raised an eyebrow. "I would have thought that was obvious."

"Well, keep them outside then."

"Gerbils aren't outside animals," I protested. "They'll die!"

Claire shrugged. "So?"

"Mom!" I wailed.

My mother shut her eyes and shook her head. Then she took a deep breath and said, "The gerbils stay."

Claire opened her mouth to argue, but Mom didn't give her the chance.

"End of discussion."

Claire threw herself on her bed.

"You can save the tantrum," Mom told her. "And don't get comfortable either. Your father and grandmother will be here in less than three hours, and I want this room spotless. If you start now, you just might get done in time. And I don't mean throw everything in the hamper either, Claire. Use the hangers — they're those wire things on the rod in the closet. When you've unburied the furniture, I want you to dust. I also expect you to change the sheets on your bed and *make* it. Then you can do the rug. I trust you remember where the vacuum is kept."

If looks could kill, my mother would have dropped dead on the spot. But she didn't. Instead, she returned Claire's icy stare with one of her own and went back to the kitchen.

So, naturally Claire took her bad mood out on me. It's hard enough living with my sister when she gets her own way, but when she doesn't, she's impossible.

"I hope you're happy," she sneered.

I didn't say anything. I didn't even look at her. I didn't want to antagonize her more than she already was. But I *did* feel a little better. I wouldn't have called it happiness exactly — it was more a feeling of victory. For once, justice had won out. I put Sandy and Sandy on top of my dresser and found new homes for the rest of my things. Then I sat down on the bed.

Claire muttered as she stormed around the room slamming drawers and throwing clothes.

"What are you staring at?" she growled at me.

I looked away and shook my head. "I'm not."

I didn't know what to do. If I continued to sit on my bed, Claire was only going to get madder, and that meant more trouble. On the other hand, if I left, she would think she could push me around and — as much as I didn't want to be there — I had to let her know it was my room too.

Luckily, Mom decided she needed my help at that moment and solved the problem for me.

.... When I'd polished the living room tables and changed the towels in the bathroom, I went looking for my mother again. Our house isn't all that big, so she shouldn't have been too hard to find, but she was whipping from room to room like a cyclone on a rampage, and it seemed wherever I went, she'd just left. Eventually I tracked her down in the dining room. She was on her hands and knees, stuffing books and papers into the bottom drawer of the buffet.

She peered up at me and shrugged guiltily. "I

don't want Gramma to see this mess, but I don't have time to sort through it right now," she said. "I'll do it later."

I didn't say anything. It was no great mystery where Claire got her untidy streak.

"What else do you want me to do?" I asked.

Mom smiled and blew a wisp of hair out of her face. Then she said, "I left a bowl of fresh flowers on the kitchen counter. Be a sweetheart and put them on the table in Gramma's bedroom, would you?"

I nodded and trundled off to the kitchen. How like my mother to think of flowers. She was always doing stuff like that. Maybe she wasn't the world's best housekeeper, but she had to have the world's biggest heart. Besides taking care of all of us, she did volunteer work at the school and the hospital — and for every good cause that came along. No matter how busy she was, she always seemed willing to take on more. My dad thought she did too much.

"Tara, if you don't slow down, you're going to get sick," he'd say sternly.

But Mom would just laugh. "Don't be ridiculous. I haven't time to be sick." And she must have been right, because I couldn't remember her even ever having a cold.

As I headed down the hall, I peeked in at Claire. She was fighting with the vacuum — and I think she was actually winning. The place was so clean, I hardly recognized it. For some reason that cheered me up.

I went into my old room and put the flowers on the table. Then I threw open the curtains. Rays of sunlight shot into the room like laser beams. I glanced around. Everything looked nice. It didn't look like my room any more, but it looked nice. I decided my grandmother should be quite comfortable. And for the first time, I felt something besides resentment at the thought of giving up my bedroom.

I must have been getting used to the idea of my grandmother moving in. In fact, the more I thought about it, the more I began to think it might be kind of fun. If nothing else, it had made Claire clean her room.

The phone rang. Mom answered it. I could hear her voice, but I couldn't make out what she was saying. Then she hung up and hollered down the hall. "Girls, that was your father. He and Gramma just landed. They'll be here in twenty minutes."

3

.... I stared out the living room window, watching for the car. My mother was still doing last-minute tidying, and Claire was holed up in the bedroom with her scissors and a magazine she'd discovered while cleaning.

I was trying to imagine what life with my grandmother was going to be like. I'd only been a year old when we'd moved from Winnipeg to Victoria, and all I had to remember Gramma by were awkward telephone conversations and a couple of whirlwind visits when I was little.

Other than a few basic facts, I didn't know her. She was my dad's mother, and her name was Fiona. I'd never heard of anybody else with that name, but according to my parents, it had been popular when my grandmother was born. She'd come from a big family, and she'd been a nurse in the army during the

Second World War. That's where she'd met Grandpa Tom. He'd been a pilot – shot down – and Gramma had taken care of him. When the war ended, they'd gotten married and had a couple of kids – Uncle Mark and my dad, Peter.

That was all I knew. I tried to recall other things, but my recollections were fuzzy, more like sensations than actual memories – split-second flashes of a small, quiet lady with white hair, Lawrence Welk reruns on the television, honeysuckle and cinnamon, a blue budgie flying free around a living room, stiff lace doilies on tables and the arms of chairs.

It wasn't much to go on. Especially since Gramma Granville was the only grandparent I had. My other grandparents had all died before I was born. I thought about my friends' grandparents. They came in a variety of shapes, sizes, and ages. Even so, they all had something in common. They were cheerful, and they doted on their grandchildren.

I smiled to myself. That could be good. I loved my parents, and they were pretty understanding about most things, but it couldn't hurt to have someone around who made a fuss about you for no reason at all and took your side even when you did something wrong.

The phone rang again. I didn't pay much attention because it's almost always for Claire. So when she shouted, "Annie, it's for you, but don't take all day!" I was surprised.

I found the phone and wandered back to the window.

"Hello?"

"Good afternoon, Miss. I represent the Lazy Neighbor Cemetery, and I am calling to offer you a once-in-a-lifetime opportunity to purchase your very own plot in our lovely, peaceful graveyard. Prices have never been better, and business is lively — NOT. People are dying to get in here, I tell ya."

"Hi, Joel," I said.

"How'd you know it was me?"

"Just a wild guess. What do you want?"

"Nice, Annie — really nice. Don't you know anything about telephone manners? You're supposed to ask me how it's going, thank me for calling — that sort of thing."

I sighed. I knew Joel would keep this up until I went along. "Sorry, Joel. How's it going? Thanks for calling. What do you want?"

"I give up," he groaned, and in my mind I could see him throwing up his hands.

But Joel and I had been friends forever. I knew him. If you wanted answers, you had to be blunt.

"Why are you calling? Shouldn't you be at baseball tryouts or something?"

"Yeah, we'll be leaving in a few minutes. I just wanted to find out if your granny arrived."

"Not yet, but my dad called to say their plane is in, so they should be here any minute."

"Are you excited?"

"A little, I guess. I'm not really sure what to expect. I don't know my grandmother very well. The last time I saw her I was only five."

"Do you think she'll bring you a present?"

"Joel!"

"What?"

"You're not supposed to say things like that. It's rude!"

"No, it's not. My granny always gives me presents. Of course, that means I have to let her pinch my cheeks and stuff, but it's usually worth it. Oh, she's given me a few duds — ugly socks and a plaid flannel shirt once — but otherwise her presents are pretty good. Lately, it's been money. You can't go wrong there."

"Joel Werner, you're awful!"

"Why? Cuz I'm honest? Don't pretend you haven't thought about it, Annie."

"I haven't!"

"Okay, fine." Obviously he didn't believe me. "So do I get an invite to tea?"

"Why?" I asked suspiciously. "Are you expecting a present?"

"Hey, you never know." At the other end of the phone, Joel was grinning. I could tell by his voice. "After-school times are best for me. Anyway, I gotta go. My dad's pointing at his watch and giving me the evil eye. Talk to ya later."

Moments later, the Werners' van emerged from the garage next door and rolled down the driveway. I waved. Joel waved back, and Mr. Werner leaned on the horn.

"Who was that?" My mom came into the living room and flopped into a chair.

"Joel and his dad," I said. "They're on their way to baseball tryouts."

Mom closed her eyes and made a mumbling noise that I took to mean, "That's nice." Then she asked, "Any sign of your father?"

I giggled.

Mom opened one eye. "What?"

I pointed at her. "You have a huge black smudge on the end of your nose and dust bunnies in your hair."

She smiled and rubbed wearily at her nose with the back of her hand. "It's my new domestic look. Do you think your grandmother will like it?"

I turned back to the window. "We'll soon find out," I said. "They're here."

.... Because Dad had already been with Gramma for a few days, he left the official welcoming duties to us and got right to work on the boxes and suitcases. I hung back and watched while Mom and Claire tripped over each other, trying to get Gramma, her purse, and her cane out of the car.

It was sort of like watching a Three Stooges movie.

When they'd finally managed it, Claire hugged Gramma and gave her a peck on the cheek. Then, as though she'd been doing it forever, she took Gramma's elbow and together they made their way slowly up the walk. I was amazed. Claire was being so nice. I hadn't realized she even knew how.

Behind them was my father, weighted down with luggage. His knees looked ready to buckle, so I hurried to help him.

"Thanks, duck," he grunted as I relieved him of a suitcase. I glanced into the open trunk. It was still half full. The back seat of the car was heaped with baggage too.

"Gramma's sure got a lot of stuff," I remarked.

"This isn't even a fraction of it. The rest is being shipped." Dad peered over his shoulder to see how I was doing. "Can you manage that thing?" he asked.

I nodded. The suitcase was large and awkward. It was also heavy. But while my father was watching, I pretended it was light as a feather. Then, gripping it tightly with both hands, I struggled up the walk behind him.

"Where is Gramma gonna put everything?" I thought about my old bedroom. It was pretty small and already crowded with furniture. The basement was jam-packed too.

Dad shook his head. "I haven't the foggiest idea."

It took four trips to empty the car. Somehow we

managed to squeeze the suitcases into the bedroom, but the boxes had to be piled in the hall.

"Good grief, Mother." Dad grimaced and rubbed his back. "Did you have the kitchen sink packed in that last one?"

To my surprise, Gramma snapped at him. "Try sorting through *your* life's belongings, and see what *you* throw away."

Dad held up his hands defensively. "Easy there, Mom. I was just kidding. Don't bite my head off the very first day."

There was an uncomfortable pause. It only lasted a few seconds, but it seemed longer. It was my mother who broke it.

"Annie, you haven't said hello to Gramma yet," she said. "Come and give her a hug."

Self-consciously, I crossed the room and wrapped my arms around my grandmother. It was like hugging cardboard. She didn't even bother to hug me back. Feeling embarrassed, I stepped away.

She glared at me with hard blue eyes. "So, Ann Elizabeth, we meet at last," she barked. It sounded like an accusation. She stared at me for another few seconds, and I smiled uneasily. I tried to think of something to say, but I was too slow. Gramma made a harumphing noise and turned away. The introduction was over.

I was relieved and disappointed at the same time. Certainly I was happy to be out of the spotlight, but it didn't seem as if my grandmother had been overly impressed with me. Why not? I was a nice person. It was Claire who was hard to get along with, and yet Gramma seemed to like her just fine. I felt an inferiority complex coming on.

I think my mother was a bit stunned by Gramma's reaction too. She tried to rebuild my image. "Annie's giving you her bedroom, Mother," she said. "It's a lovely little room with a wonderful view of the backyard."

Gramma looked at me again, and I became instantly uneasy.

"You volunteered, did you?" Her eyes narrowed suspiciously. "Or did your parents do the volunteering for you?"

Suddenly I felt guilty. As if reading my mind, Mom put her arm around me and drew me close.

"Oh, Mother, don't be silly. Annie is a very generous person." I thought I heard Claire snort, but then Mom was talking again. "You just wait until you get to know her. You'll see for yourself. I have a feeling you two are going to be the best of friends." Then she gave my shoulder a squeeze and added, "Isn't that right, sweetheart?"

I was beginning to feel like a Ping-Pong ball.

"We'll see." Gramma didn't seem convinced, but she didn't argue.

"Can I get you a cup of tea, Mother?" my mom put in quickly before Gramma could find anything else wrong with me.

"Good idea. Cream, no sugar. And not that skimmed nonsense either. I like real milk in my tea."

"I'll do it," Claire volunteered unexpectedly, and headed for the kitchen.

"I'll help," I mumbled, and hurried after her, grateful for a chance to escape the tension in the living room.

Like a robot, I arranged the teacups on a tray and filled a plate with cookies. Claire was ragging at me about something, but I was more concerned with the old lady in the other room. If first impressions counted for anything, I was in big trouble. Gramma Granville didn't like me. And I wasn't all that sure I was crazy about her either. My parents may have meant well, but that didn't take away the sick feeling in the pit of my stomach. I had been right all along — this wasn't going to work.

4

.... "And they like to chew. Paper towel and toilet-tissue rolls are their favorites. Okay?" I waited for some sign that Joel had heard me, and when he nodded, I went on. "And make really, really, *really* sure that they always have water."

Joel nodded again.

"You won't forget?" Water was the most important thing.

This time Joel shook his head. "I won't forget."

But I didn't feel any better. "Here's their food." I heaved an enormous plastic bag onto the table with a thud. "Don't let their dish get empty."

"I won't, Annie. I promise. Trust me, I'll take good care of your gerbils."

Not as good as me, I thought, but I couldn't very well say that to Joel.

"Hey, cool!" he grinned, digging his hand into

the plastic bag. "Sunflower seeds. Me and Sandy and Sandy can have lunch together. I love sunflower seeds." He popped a couple into his mouth. Then he made a face and spit them back out. "*Yuck*. They're not salted."

"Of course not." I scowled at him. "Gerbils can't eat salted sunflower seeds — *only* these ones, or they'll get sick." This was terrible. Joel didn't know anything about looking after gerbils. "Are you sure you can do this?" I asked skeptically.

"Annie, stop worrying. I'm not a total moron, you know. If I can take care of a dog, I'm sure I can look after your —"

"And that's another thing," I interrupted. "You have to make sure your dog doesn't come anywhere near Sandy and Sandy."

"Aw, Annie, you know Samson wouldn't hurt a fly," Joel objected.

"But he's so big, he might scare them to death or something." My mind was racing. I was sure I was forgetting something important.

"Will you stop worrying? It's not like you're moving to the North Pole, you know. You're right next door. They're still your gerbils." Then Joel grinned again. "You just have to come over here to clean their cage."

I sank onto a chair. I was miserable. "I hate this," I moaned. "First I lose my bedroom and now my gerbils. It's not fair! I wish my grandmother had never come to live with us."

Joel looked surprised. He was the one who usually said that sort of thing — not me.

"It's not your granny's fault she has musophobia," he said. Ever since Joel did a research report on phobias, he considered himself an expert.

"What the heck is musophobia?" I scowled.

"It's the fear of mice —" I opened my mouth to protest, but Joel didn't give me a chance "— but I'm pretty sure it includes gerbils too."

I scowled harder.

"As for your bedroom," he shrugged, "well, you can't expect your granny to sleep on the couch, can you?"

I knew Joel was right, but I resented him taking my grandmother's side.

"No," I admitted. "I know it's nobody's fault, but that doesn't mean I can't hate it. You should have seen Claire when she found out I had to get rid of my gerbils. She positively gloated."

"Didn't your mom and dad give her heck?"

"Oh, sure, but what good does that do?"

Joel nodded. "True."

I knew he was trying to be sympathetic, but I had the feeling Joel thought I was making this a bigger deal than it was. That's because it wasn't happening to him.

"You know what really bugs me?" I said.

"What's that?"

"It's like it's all for nothing."

"What is?"

"*Everything!*" The word exploded out of me, and Joel's eyebrows shot up. I continued more quietly. "Everything about my grandmother coming to live with us — me losing my bedroom and my gerbils, furniture getting shuffled around — everything! The house is practically bursting, it has so much in it. And I don't even recognize half the stuff. There are pill bottles everywhere and we even have safety handles on the bathtub now. And the worst part is that nobody is acting normal."

Joel's eyebrows relaxed, but he looked puzzled. "What do you mean?"

"Well, it's like we're on our best behavior all the time — even Claire. Everything is for Gramma. *Get Gramma a cup of tea. Turn the television down because Gramma is sleeping. Don't let Gramma hear you arguing.* Etcetera, etcetera. And nobody laughs. It's like Gramma is going to die if we have any fun. Maybe it wouldn't be so bad if all this tiptoeing around made her happy. But it doesn't! She has to be the grumpiest person I've ever met. I haven't seen her smile once!"

"You're exaggerating," Joel said.

But I wasn't. "All day long she sits on the couch in the living room and stares out the window, looking like a ferocious cigarette-smoking gargoyle."

"Your grandmother smokes?" Joel's eyebrows

jumped up again.

"Like a chimney." Just thinking about it, I could smell the smoke. I wrinkled my nose. "The whole house stinks like a dirty ashtray."

"Don't your parents mind?"

"What can they do? My grandmother's eighty-one years old. They can't very well send her out to the back porch every time she wants a cigarette. She'd be out there all the time."

There was a long pause as Joel thought about what I'd told him. Finally he said, "I'm sure things will get better. It hasn't even been two weeks. You're still getting used to each other." Then he grinned and punched me in the shoulder. "Before you know it, you and Claire will be fighting just like usual. And I wouldn't be a bit surprised if you even get your grandmother to quit smoking."

I really wanted Joel to be right, but I was sure he wasn't.

Then he changed the subject. "Have you finished that social studies assignment?"

Instantly I forgot about my grandmother. "Yes," I drawled and made a face. "Wasn't it stupid?"

"Did you think so?"

I blinked. "Didn't you?"

Joel shrugged. "I thought it was okay."

I couldn't believe he was serious. "Oh, come on, Joel. Mrs. Pauls would never have given us an assignment like that."

Joel shrugged again. "Yeah, so?"

"So it was dumb! It must have been Mr. Brockhurst's idea." Just saying the man's name left a bad taste in my mouth.

"What if it was?"

"He's a substitute teacher!" I pointed out the obvious. "He's supposed to teach the stuff Mrs. Pauls says, not make up his own."

"Maybe he had to make up his own," Joel suggested. "Mrs. Pauls has been away all week. She's probably too sick to plan lessons."

Suddenly I felt uneasy. "What makes you think she's sick?" I asked warily. "Maybe she's at a conference or something."

Joel shook his head. "Uh-uh. If she knew she was going to be away, she would have told us. She's sick, all right."

I hadn't thought about that. It made sense, but I didn't like the idea at all.

"Well, I hope she gets better soon." I poked a sunflower seed through the bars of the cage and watched as one of the gerbils cracked it open. "I hate Mr. Brockhurst."

"Why? He's nice."

I could have thumped Joel. First he had defended my grandmother, and now Mr. Brockhurst. "He's not Mrs. Pauls." I glowered at Joel, but he didn't notice.

"That doesn't mean he can't be nice."

"Traitor." I sent Joel my dirtiest look, but he just laughed. Of course, that made me madder than ever. "What's so funny?" I demanded.

"You are." Joel was grinning. "There's not a thing the matter with Mr. Brockhurst. He's a good teacher and he's a nice guy. The only reason you don't like him is because he's not Mrs. Pauls."

"Mrs. Pauls is the best teacher in the whole world!"

"And you could be the president of her fan club."

I glared harder at Joel, and finally it seemed to have some effect.

"Fine," he conceded, rolling his eyes. "Have it your way. I should know better than to argue with you when you're in this kind of mood."

"I'm not in any kind of a mood," I grumbled. "I just want my *real* teacher back."

Joel sighed. "Well, don't have a fit about it. She'll probably be back tomorrow."

.... But she wasn't.

Not only did Mrs. Pauls *not* return to school the next day, but right after morning recess, Mr. Watson, the principal, came into our classroom and told us she wouldn't be back for the rest of the year! I felt like I'd been punched in the stomach. I think I even stopped breathing for a few seconds. Mr. Watson said it was a medical problem, but that we shouldn't worry because Mrs. Pauls would be as good as new by September.

September! I'd be in grade seven by then. And that meant I would never be in Mrs. Pauls' class again! I was devastated. This wasn't supposed to happen. Mrs. Pauls was the best teacher in the whole school, and I had waited years to be in her class.

Mr. Watson was still talking, so I made myself concentrate on what he was saying.

"... has done a fine job covering for Mrs. Pauls this week. I think you should show him your appreciation." Most of the kids clapped. I didn't. Mr. Watson continued with his speech. "Substituting on a long-term basis is a bit different, however. Fortunately for us, Mr. Brockhurst has indicated he is up to the challenge. Therefore, I am happy to inform you that he will be your teacher for the remainder of the year."

I felt sick. As if losing Mrs. Pauls hadn't been bad enough. There was no way I could survive three whole months with Mr. Brockhurst! I would rather die. I probably *would* die!

.... I opened the front door as quietly as I could and tiptoed into the house. Then I listened. There was no television noise. No voices either. I sniffed the air. It reeked of stale cigarettes, but there was no smoke. I crossed my fingers. Maybe my grandmother was napping.

I hoped so. I wasn't in the mood for her daily interrogation. Not that it ever lasted long. Gramma didn't seem very interested in my activities — or me, for that matter. Just the same, those after-school "talks" always left me feeling sore, as if I'd been poked all over with a knitting needle.

I tried to peer into the living room without being seen. But I couldn't see around the corner. I leaned in a little further.

"Ann Elizabeth? What are you doing skulking in the hallway?"

Rats! Reluctantly I let myself into the room. The last thing I felt like doing was smiling, but I tried.

My grandmother eyed me suspiciously. "You look like you're in pain, child," she said. "Do you have a stomachache?"

I shook my head and sat down on the chair across from her.

"No homework?" She reached for a cigarette and matches.

"Not today, Gramma," I said. My voice sounded dead, even to me.

"Why not?" My grandmother didn't waste any time getting on my case. "There's always something you could be learning. Are you so smart that you don't need to study? The devil finds mischief for idle hands, you know. That's what my dead father used to say." Then she struck a match and put it up to the cigarette in her mouth. But, as usual, she held it too far away, and though she puffed and puffed, she couldn't get the cigarette to light.

I watched the match burn away.

"Blasted thing!" Gramma exclaimed as it singed her fingers. She let it go, and it fell to the rug.

I jumped off my chair and snatched it up. The flame had gone out and a ribbon of smoke spiraled from the shriveled black stem. I dropped it into the ashtray and knelt down to gather up the charred remains of a number of other matches.

I held out my hand. "Look at these," I frowned. "There have to be six or seven dead matches here, Gramma. Do you know how dangerous that is? You could light yourself on fire. You could light the whole house on fire!"

She didn't seem to care. "Nonsense and poppycock." She waved me away and reached for a new match. "I've been smoking for over sixty years, and I'm still here, aren't I? They just don't make matches like they used to."

"Well, then why don't you use the lighter Dad gave you?" I asked, looking around the table for it. "It's a lot safer than matches."

"I can't get it to work. It's one of those new-fangled gadgets," she scowled.

"It's child-proofed," I explained as I flicked it and lit her cigarette. "Look. I'll show you how it works."

But Gramma pushed me away, and there was irritation in her voice as she growled, "I'll never remember that."

I put the lighter back on the table. What was the use? Nothing I said was going to make my grandmother change her mind. Not only was she the grumpiest person I'd ever met, she was also the most stubborn. *A bit set in her ways* — that's how my mother put it. But all the sugary words in the world couldn't change the facts. Gramma Granville was a cranky, bull-headed old woman.

Nothing seemed to make her happy, and I couldn't help wondering if she had to work at being in a bad mood all the time. She seemed to find fault in everything and everyone — especially my mother. That really bugged me, because my mom tried so hard to please her.

"You don't have much to say for yourself today," Gramma remarked. As usual, it sounded like a criticism. If I'd been full of news, she would have jumped all over me for talking too much. I couldn't win.

"I'm a little depressed, I guess," I mumbled. It was true, but I had no idea why I was telling my grandmother. It was almost guaranteed she wouldn't be sympathetic.

"Depressed! *Ha*!" she cackled, and I instantly regretted my confession. "Little girl like you — what do you have to be depressed about? You have your whole life ahead of you. That's the trouble with you young people — you don't know when you're well off. To you, life is one big holiday. You have no responsibilities, no worries. Fast this, fast that. You want something, your parents buy it for you. You don't have to work at anything. But stub your toe and suddenly you're depressed." Then she wagged her finger at me. "Don't talk to me about depression. Wait until you get old. Then you'll have something to be depressed about."

As she spoke, I could feel anger bubbling up inside me until I was like a volcano about to erupt.

Gramma Granville was so mean and insensitive! A person didn't have to be old to have problems. Didn't she know that? I wasn't even twelve yet, and I had more troubles than I knew what to do with — like losing my bedroom and being forced to give up my gerbils. And now, the best teacher I'd ever had was gone, replaced by someone I couldn't stand! But my grandmother wouldn't care about that.

For a few very long seconds, I gripped the arms of the chair with all my might as I fought to hold my feelings inside. Then, when I thought I could speak without screaming, I stood up and said, "I better let Mom know I'm home," and ran out of the room.

My mother was in the kitchen, stirring a pot on the stove and talking on the telephone. I glanced around the room. Books and papers were scattered over the table and chairs. Cupboard doors were flung wide, and partially unpacked grocery bags covered the counters. A plant in the process of being repotted sat on newspaper in the middle of the floor.

Mom smiled and rolled her eyes at the phone propped between her ear and shoulder.

"Yes, Mrs. Morton, that's right," she was saying. "We exceeded our fundraising goal by over a thousand dollars, thanks to the efforts of volunteers like you. Naturally, we hope to do even better this year. Can we count on your help? Wonderful! Let me see what's still available." She waved at me to pass her one of the papers from the table. "Okay. I have the list right here. Yes, the area around Royal Oak Shopping Center is still open if you'd like ..."

I wished my mother would hurry up and finish her call. I needed to talk to her. She'd understand how I felt.

I wandered over to the counter and rummaged through the grocery bags — canned goods, fruit, potatoes, crackers, ice cream. I reached for the ice cream carton. It was barely cold, and it was squishy. I pulled it out. Something gooey and brown began to ooze from the bottom. I plunked the carton into the sink and wiped up the mess. Then I put away the rest of the groceries.

Finally Mom hung up the phone. She peeked under the lids of a couple of pots and then started riffling through the papers on the table.

"Can I talk to you, Mom?" I asked, and she jumped.

"Annie!" she exclaimed, grabbing a chair and her chest at the same time. "I didn't realize you were still here. You scared the life out of me." Then she smiled. "I guess I'm a little preoccupied. The day has been crazy. I've been running around like a chicken with my head cut off." She turned back to the pile of papers on the table again. "How was *your* day?" she asked, but the way she said it, I could tell her mind was somewhere else.

"We had a Martian visit our class," I said.

"That's nice," she mumbled, picking up the phone

once more. Then one of the pots on the stove started boiling over. "Oh, no!" she exclaimed, dropping the phone and racing for a potholder.

I sighed and headed for the bedroom.

Claire was there with two of her friends. Conversation stopped as soon as I walked through the door. I could feel three pairs of eyes follow me to my side of the room.

As I went to sit down, Claire snapped, "Don't you have somewhere else to go, Annie? We're trying to have a private conversation here."

I glared back at her, but I didn't have the energy to argue. It wouldn't have made a difference anyway.

"And don't listen at the door," Claire barked as I shut it.

"Like I care about your dumb gossip," I muttered, and started down the hall. Then I stopped. Where was I going? Mom obviously didn't have time for me, so there was no point going back to the kitchen. The living room meant Gramma, and I definitely didn't want that. I could go next door, but I didn't really feel like talking to Joel at the moment.

I let myself out the back door, wandered around to the front of the house and flopped down on the steps. I was still there when my dad's car pulled into the driveway half an hour later.

"Why so glum, chum?" he asked as he made his way up the walk. "It's too nice a day for such a long face. Did you lose your best friend or what?"

That was all the encouragement I needed. I had to tell someone about Mrs. Pauls, so like a bottle popping its cork, I blurted the latest of the disasters in my life.

"And I don't even have anywhere I can go to think about stuff any more," I finished with a whine. "Gramma has *my* room *and* the living room, Mom is all over the *kitchen*, and Claire hardly lets me through the door of *her* bedroom — even though it's supposed to belong to *both* of us now." I'd been emphasizing every second word. When Dad chuckled, I had to smile too.

He ruffled my hair. "Don't let it get you down, duck. I know what Claire can be like, but hang in there. Don't let her push you around. It's your room too. As far as the situation with Mrs. Pauls goes ..." He shrugged. "It's too bad, but there's really nothing you can do about it. Unfortunately, that sort of thing happens. But try to keep an open mind. You might find that this Mr. Brockhurst isn't such a bad guy after all."

That wasn't what I wanted to hear.

6

......................................I don't think I said two words during dinner that night. I was too busy thinking about my life — the way it was falling apart one piece at a time, and how there was nothing I could do about it. I wasn't asking for anything more than what I'd always had — my room, my gerbils, my teacher. But in just a couple of weeks, I'd lost them all.

I scowled across the table at my grandmother. This was *her* fault. If she hadn't come to live with us, things would be like they'd always been. I would still have my own bedroom, and my gerbils wouldn't be at Joel's house. I thought about Mrs. Pauls and Mr. Brockhurst. I couldn't honestly blame my grandmother for that problem — but I would have liked to.

My scowl turned to a grimace as Gramma pulled a half-eaten carrot out of her mouth and plopped it back onto her dinner plate. Then she frowned at my mother and complained, "These carrots are tough. Why don't you cook your vegetables properly, Tara?"

I hadn't been very hungry before, but the sight of that partly chewed carrot killed my appetite completely.

It was my father who replied. "The carrots are fine, Mother. If you'd put your teeth in, you would find it makes a world of difference." He had a smile on his face, but something told me he wasn't laughing.

"I do have my teeth in," Gramma snapped.

"*All* of them, Mother."

"I don't need all of them. The bottom ones are uncomfortable, and I can manage just fine with my uppers — *if* the food is cooked properly."

My dad went to say something else, but Mom spoke up first. "I'm sorry, Mother," she apologized. "I keep forgetting you like your vegetables more well done."

"It isn't a matter of well done, my girl," Gramma retorted. "These aren't cooked at all." She gave the carrot a disgusted flick with her fork. "How can you people eat them?"

"With teeth." Dad shoved another forkful of carrots into his mouth and chewed noisily.

"*Hmmph*," Gramma sniffed, turning back to her dinner. "At least the potatoes are cooked."

The dinner-table discussion moved on, but I wasn't listening. I was watching my grandmother. What *had* happened to her teeth? She'd arrived with a mouthful of them, but I hadn't seen them since. Well, not in her face, anyway. Except for mealtimes, they sat in a glass of water on the windowsill in the bathroom.

The telephone rang, and Claire jumped up from the table. "I'll get it," she announced, tearing into the hall.

"Whoever it is, tell them you'll call back," Dad shouted after her. "You aren't done with your dinner."

"May I be excused?" I said, turning to my mother. "I'm not very hungry."

She didn't answer me. Her body was there, but her mind obviously wasn't. I waved a hand in front of her face.

"What?" she said as her eyes focused again. "Sorry, Annie. I was thinking about something else. What did you say?"

"I asked to be excused."

Mom looked at my plate.

"You haven't finished your dinner." Then she smiled. "And there's apple pie for dessert." But I shook my head. Her smile faded. "What's the matter? Aren't you feeling well?"

Claire slid back into her chair and began eating again.

"So who called?" Dad asked. "Obviously it wasn't for you, or you'd still be on the phone."

Claire gave him a dirty look. "It was for Annie."

"Thanks for telling me," I grumbled.

"Hey, if I can't take phone calls during dinner, neither can you," she sniped.

"Who was it?"

Claire shrugged and pushed more food into her mouth.

"Didn't you even *ask*?"

She looked at me as if I was an annoying ant. "Who do you think it was? There's only one person who ever calls you."

I gritted my teeth and turned to my mother again. "May I *please* be excused?" When Mom nodded, I pushed my chair away from the table and ran for the phone.

"It's me," I said when Joel picked up. "Why'd you call?"

There was a pause before he said, "I have some good news and I have some bad news."

I wasn't in the mood for games. "Could you just —"

"Which do you want first?"

I was already frustrated, but there was no point in arguing.

"The bad," I conceded.

"Are you sure?"

"Joel! If you have something to say — *say it*! Or else I'm going to hang up."

"Sandy and Sandy escaped."

"What!" I almost dropped the phone.

"Now ask me the good news."

I couldn't believe him. He'd lost my gerbils, and he was still playing games!

"My gerbils escaped!" I shouted. "How? Where? Joel

Werner, I trusted you. You said you'd take good —"

"I *said*, ask me the good news."

"I don't care about your good news!" I yelled. "I care about my gerbils. Where —"

"Ask me the good news!" Joel shouted back. "The good news is good, Annie. Ask me!" Then suddenly he gave in. "Oh, what's the use? It's a joke. I was kidding. Sandy and Sandy didn't escape. They're fine. All they were doing was playing under my bed while I cleaned their cage. They chewed a hole in one of my socks — my mom wasn't real happy about that — but otherwise ..."

I didn't hear the rest. I was already racing across the backyard to Joel's house.

.... I snuggled Sandy and Sandy to my cheek. They were soft and warm and very wiggly. They kept sniffing the air and trying to climb across my shoulders. Running free around Joel's bedroom had gotten them all wound up.

"You see?" Joel said. "I told you. They're fine."

Unfortunately, I wasn't. I was still upset. "Something *could* have happened," I pointed out crossly. "What if they'd gotten out of your room? What if Samson had caught them? What if —"

Joel shook his head vigorously. "Uh-uh. Nothing could've happened. I shut the bedroom door before I opened their cage, and Samson was out in the yard.

Sandy and Sandy went exploring. That's all. You can see for yourself — they're perfectly all right. So stop having a fit. It was just a little joke. *Man*, if I'd known you were going to flip out like this, I never would've phoned you."

Joel was right. I had overreacted; I just didn't want to admit it. I put the gerbils back in their cage and made a big show of closing the door securely.

Right away, Sandy and Sandy began rearranging the clean wood shavings and burrowing through the twin toilet tissue rolls Joel had put inside. I examined the cage carefully. The food dish was full. So was the water bottle. Newspaper lined the bottom of the cage beneath the shavings. I couldn't find a thing wrong with Joel's cleaning job. That should have made me feel better, but it didn't.

"I'm sorry you can't keep Sandy and Sandy at your house," he said. "I know coming to see them here isn't the same."

I could feel my anger melting away. If Joel was going to be nice to me, I was going to cry.

"Well, it's better than not seeing them at all," I said gruffly, concentrating on the gerbils' antics to keep the tears away. And then I realized that what I had said was true. It *was* better! If it weren't for Joel, I would have had to give up my gerbils altogether. Joel was doing me a favor, and I was criticizing him. Suddenly I felt guilty. "Thanks for taking care of them," I mumbled.

"No problem." Joel's grin was infectious, and I smiled back.

"Want to watch some television after?" he asked as we began putting away the gerbil supplies.

"Sure," I said. I hadn't watched much television since my grandmother had moved in. She talked through all the programs. "Where do you want this newspaper?" I pointed to the pages strewn over the floor.

Joel looked around. "With the wood shavings, I guess."

I began gathering up the loose sheets, but a headline caught my attention, and soon my eyes were racing across the words, and my heart was thumping in my chest.

I jumped to my feet. "Oh, no!"

Joel spun around. "What's the matter?"

"Oh, no!" I cried again. "No, no, no! This is horrible!"

"What?" Joel demanded, trying to read the paper I was waving in the air.

I felt as if I'd just fallen through a trapdoor into a cold, dark hole. I threw the newspaper down and sagged against the wall.

Joel retrieved it and began hunting for the article that had set me off.

"What were you reading?" he frowned.

All I could do was stare at him. I felt flat, like Wile E. Coyote when Road Runner barrels over him with a steam-roller. Except Wile E. Coyote always pops back into shape, and I didn't think I was going to.

"Annie?"

"*Long-time Historical Society Disbands.*" My voice sounded like it belonged to someone else. "That reenactment group I've been waiting to join — History Repeats Itself — it's breaking up."

Joel hunted down the article and read it. Then he turned back to me. "Hey, Annie, I'm really sorry."

I tried to smile, but I couldn't. "You know," I said, "I've been waiting two years to join that group. Two whole years, and in a few more weeks I would have been old enough. If you haven't seen a reenactment, you wouldn't understand, but it's kind of like traveling in a time machine. And *I* was going to do it!" Then I heard myself snort. "It figures. Every time I turn around lately, something else is going wrong. Maybe I should just lie on the road and let a bus run me over." I sank onto the end of Joel's bed. "No. That wouldn't work either. The bus would probably run out of gas before it hit me."

Joel tried to cheer me up. "So you're having a little bad luck right now. It can't last."

"A *little*!" I shouted, startling both of us. "If I didn't have bad luck, I wouldn't have any luck at all!"

Joel tried again. "Don't let it get you down. Things have to start improving soon."

I let out a huge, frustrated sigh and fell full out onto the bed. "Well, they sure couldn't get any worse."

Boy, was I wrong.

.... The next disaster struck two days later.

My father got a promotion. I know that doesn't sound like a bad thing, but right away he started working twelve-hour days. It felt weird sitting down to supper without him. It was so quiet. And the food was different too. Since Dad was having his evening meal at work, Mom had begun cooking to please Gramma, and we were eating things like scrambled eggs and shepherd's pie — stuff that slid down your throat without being chewed.

Most nights Dad didn't get home until around nine o'clock. That was only half an hour before I had to go to bed, so suddenly I wasn't seeing very much of him at all. As if that wasn't bad enough, lacrosse season had started, and we weren't getting to any of the Shamrocks' games. Dad and I are huge lacrosse fans, and we always have season's tickets. But not this year. My father was so busy with work, I don't think he even realized the season was underway.

"I'll go to the games with you if you want," Joel offered when we were having a snack at his house after school one day.

"You don't like lacrosse," I reminded him. I poked at the chocolate cake on my plate. It was good, but I wasn't hungry. "Besides, part of the fun of the games is going with my dad. No offense," I added quickly. It was nice of Joel to volunteer, and I didn't want him to think I was ungrateful.

"What about your sister?" Joel asked. "Does she like lacrosse?"

"Claire?" I snorted. "She doesn't know a lacrosse stick from a baseball bat. She came once last year and spent the whole time checking out the guys. The only way she'd ever go to a game with me is if I paid her about a hundred dollars, and even then I'd have to sit somewhere else and pretend I didn't know her."

"What about your mom?"

I shook my head. "No. She'd probably come if I asked her, but it's not really her kind of thing. Besides, with my dad working such long hours, she's busier than ever. If she's not in the kitchen, she's helping my grandmother with something or working for one of her charities. Now that the weather is nice, she's up to her eyeballs in gardening too. I'd feel guilty asking her to take me to a lacrosse game."

"You never know. Maybe she'd like a break," Joel suggested.

"I don't think so," I said. "The other day my dad came home from work early — for once — and told my mom to get dressed up, because he was taking her out to dinner. He said they'd both been working way too hard and deserved a break. But my mom said all she wanted to do was have a nice long bath and go to bed."

"Did your dad go out to dinner anyway?"

I shook my head. "Uh-uh. He fell asleep in his chair."

.... It seemed strange that I should have told Joel that story considering what happened the next day.

I came in from school to find the house empty except for my grandmother. It wasn't the first time my mother had been out when I'd come home, so I assumed she was running errands or doing her volunteer work. But when both my parents walked in forty minutes later, I knew right away that something was wrong.

I followed them into the kitchen. Mom dropped her coat onto a chair and, without saying a word, began rummaging through the refrigerator.

"Medication and plenty of rest." Dad shook a bottle of pills at her and scowled. "You heard the doctor, Tara. You're suffering from exhaustion. You have to slow down. We just walked in the front door, for heaven's sake, and already you're tearing around like a crazy woman."

I was stunned. Was my mother sick? She couldn't be — she was never sick. I studied her carefully. She did look tired. She was pale, and there were dark smudges beneath her eyes. She seemed thin too. Why hadn't I noticed those things before? *Exhaustion*, Dad had said. I had no idea what that was, but it didn't sound good. Especially if it involved medicine.

My mother glanced sideways at Dad and continued pulling food out of the refrigerator. "I am not tearing around," she sighed. "Don't be so dramatic. I am making dinner."

But Dad didn't listen to her. Instead, he took her by the arm and led her to a chair.

"Sit," he said.

"Peter, don't be ridiculous. I have —"

"Sit," he repeated in his no-nonsense voice.

Mom shook her head wearily and sank onto the kitchen chair. Then Dad pulled another chair over and eased her legs onto it.

He was making such a fuss — my mother really must be sick. I began to feel uneasy.

"There," Dad said, with an air of finality, "that's much better. Now, how about a cup of tea?"

Mom went to put her feet down, but my father stopped her.

"Peter, I feel silly," she said. "You're sweet, really, but this isn't necessary. I'm fine. Now let me get up. I have to make supper."

My mother still *sounded* like she was all right.

But Dad didn't give in. "No, you don't. Not tonight. The girls can make supper."

"Peter, you're overreacting. I'm not that bad — just a little tired. It isn't going to kill me to cook a meal."

Suddenly it dawned on me how we all took my mother for granted. She did everything for everyone, and we let her. I felt guilty. "No, Mom," I heard myself saying as I crossed the room. "Dad's right. You *should* have a rest. You work way too hard. Claire and I can make supper."

"Thank you, Annie." She smiled and patted my hand. "I appreciate the offer, sweetie, but —"

"Then it's settled." Dad crossed his arms over his chest and yelled for Claire.

Kraft Dinner and grilled cheese sandwiches — it wasn't the kind of supper that Mom would have made, but my parents said it was great. For once, my grandmother didn't say anything.

8

.... After that, Dad, Claire and I took over the housework. Claire and I did the vacuuming, dusting, and general tidying. Dad cut his overtime back to a couple of days a week and took on the laundry, marketing, and gardening. For a few days the three of us even took turns getting dinner, but when Mom insisted that cooking one meal a day wasn't going to tire her, we gave in almost right away. Dad did make her give up her volunteer work, though – at least until the doctor said she was up to it again. But the one thing we couldn't help with was Gramma. Since we were away all day, my mother was still the one looking after her. She never complained, but it was easy to tell she wasn't getting the rest she needed. It really bugged me that my grandmother didn't try to do more for herself, and because of that I resented her more than ever.

My birthday came and went. If it hadn't been for the gifts from my parents and the card from Joel, I could have forgotten it completely. I almost wished I had. A few weeks earlier, I had really been looking forward to this birthday. But now that History Repeats Itself had folded, turning twelve didn't matter to me any more.

Actually, nothing seemed to matter.

So much had happened in such a short time that I couldn't even work up the energy to be upset. It was like I'd been carrying around a ton of bricks for months, and the constant weight had worn me down. I couldn't help wondering if that was how my mother felt. I even considered the possibility that maybe I'd caught her exhaustion. But I knew that kind of thing wasn't contagious, and, deep down, I also knew I wasn't really tired.

I was discouraged, disillusioned, depressed — one of those *D* words — and I couldn't seem to snap out of it. I didn't even feel like writing in my school journal any more, even though Mr. Brockhurst gave us time for it every day.

If I'd been a different kind of person, I might have made a big fuss about all the things that had gone wrong, just to get them out of my system. I might even have given my grandmother a piece of my mind. It probably wouldn't have changed anything, but it might have made me feel better.

I sighed and wound up the alarm clock. Throwing

a fit was Claire's style, not mine. I just wanted life to be peaceful and smooth.

I glanced around the messy bedroom. Well, my life certainly wasn't peaceful and smooth any more. In fact, it was so jumbled, I hardly recognized it.

I looked at the clock in my hands and thought about the way things used to be.

In my old bedroom, I'd never needed an alarm. I'd had Sandy and Sandy, and it was the rustling in their cage that had woken me up every morning. But instead of getting up, I would burrow deeper under my covers and drift in and out of sleep, waiting for the rest of the house to waken. Eventually Mom would tap at the door, and that's when I would get up.

In the kitchen, things would be hectic — all of us heading in different directions at the same time, wolfing down cereal and juice, grabbing lunches and rushing out the door. Then I'd call on Joel and we'd walk to school.

Back then I'd really loved school. Mrs. Pauls was so great. She had a way of making every subject interesting — even the ones that weren't — and the school day would be over before I knew it.

After school I would do my homework and maybe wander over to Joel's house until supper. In the evening I'd watch television or play Scrabble with my family and then climb into bed and dream about joining History Repeats Itself.

Well, that was then and this is now, I reminded

myself. Everything had changed. With Mrs. Pauls gone, school was no fun any more. And I didn't even have History Repeats Itself to look forward to. A declining membership had put an end to that.

I put the clock back on the dresser. I couldn't help wondering if Sandy and Sandy were Joel's alarm now, and that bothered me. They were *my* gerbils, but they'd been at his house so long they probably didn't even remember who I was any more.

Hot tears sprang to my eyes. I tried to blink them away, but they wouldn't go, so I sopped them up with my comforter. More than anything, I wanted to run to my mother and bawl my eyes out. But I knew I couldn't. Mom needed rest, not more problems.

Of course, that made me think about Gramma, and my tears instantly dried up. It was her fault my mother was sick. She'd worn Mom out. It made me so angry that every muscle in my body became tense.

Gramma Granville was an awful person — not anything like the warm-hearted lady in my father's stories about his growing-up years. It didn't make any sense. If my grandmother had been a different kind of person once, what had happened to change her?

I thought of my own mother again and felt myself scowling. Whatever Fiona Granville had been like before, she was a horrible old woman now. She'd invaded our home, upset our lives and made my mother sick.

It was hard to believe she'd only been living with

us for a little over two months. It felt like so much longer. What if she *never* moved out?

The thought deflated me more than ever.

"I hate you," I muttered under my breath. And I meant it. "I hate you and I wish you'd never come here." I knew it was wrong to think that, but I couldn't help how I felt, and I wasn't sorry.

9

.... "This isn't working out," I heard my father say. His voice was quiet but firm. "When we first discussed my mother moving in with us, I knew it was going to take some getting used to, but I wasn't expecting things to be this bad."

I had been about to turn into the garage, but when I heard that, I stopped short and pressed myself flat against the outside wall to listen.

"We're still adjusting," my mother whispered back. "I know things aren't perfect, but they're getting better all the time."

"How can you say that — you, of all people?" My dad obviously didn't agree. And neither did I. "You know as well as I do that she is a very big part of why you're sick right now."

So I wasn't the only one who thought that. My ears perked up even more.

"Who's next? The girls and I don't have your stamina. We're already getting frazzled," Dad went on. "And, to be quite frank, I'm not sure it's worth it."

I couldn't see into the garage, but Mom must have given my father some kind of look, because he sounded almost apologetic when he started to speak again.

"I didn't mean that like it sounded," he said. "All I'm saying is that the kids and I are getting worn out trying to do your work — and for what? You're still not getting the rest you need. All day long you're jumping up and down for Mother. At this rate, you're never going to get well."

"It's not that bad."

"Yes, it is," Dad argued. "For one thing, you're not strong enough to be hoisting her in and out of the bathtub and up and down stairs. One of these days you're both going to go for a tumble. But it's not just that. There are other things."

"Such as?"

"You wait on her hand and foot, Tara. For instance, you have shown her how to operate the remote control for the television fifty times if you've shown her once, yet whenever she wants to turn the set on, she calls you. And you go!" My father fairly shouted the last bit, and my mother shushed him.

"This can't go on." Dad was whispering again, but I could tell he was still upset.

"Be serious," my mother hissed back. "I can't ignore her. She is eighty-one years old! She needs help."

There was a pause, and I listened hard for any sign that my parents were coming out of the garage. I didn't want to be caught eavesdropping. Then I heard my father sigh, and I relaxed a little.

"I know she does. I guess I'm just wishing she didn't. It's so hard to watch her get old."

"Of course it is," Mom said sympathetically. "But if it's tough on us, just think how it must be for her."

Dad sighed again. "It's not fair. You spend your entire life trying to get by, and what's your reward? You get old and feeble. You lose your teeth, your hair, your memory — your independence. My dad was only sixty-seven when he died, but in a way I think he was lucky. He didn't go through this. Neither did your folks. But it's not like that for my mother. Old age has robbed her of her identity. You know, I look at her sometimes — sitting in the living room for hours on end like she does with her cigarettes and her thoughts — and it dawns on me that I don't even know her any more. Not only that, but it seems like every day it's becoming harder and harder to remember what she used to be like. Do you know how that makes me feel?"

There was a pause, and I thought my mother must have been shaking her head. Then Dad continued, and his voice was much louder.

"Angry! That's how it makes me feel. That's right. It makes me angry — like it's her fault she got old. Isn't that terrible? I can't even believe it myself. So then I feel guilty, but that doesn't help either. I'm a grown man. Why am I having so much trouble coming to terms with this?"

I waited for my mother to say something, but she didn't.

And then my dad was talking again. "My mother was always so busy and full of energy. Hard as it is to believe now, she was also one of the most caring and thoughtful people I've ever met. She was a lot like you, actually."

My mother chuckled. "But a better housekeeper — right?"

Dad laughed too, but I didn't see the joke. He'd said Gramma had been like my mother. How could that be? My mother was considerate and kind — and she liked to laugh! Gramma was grumpy and stubborn. But if what my father had said was true, did that mean Mom was going to end up like Gramma when she got old? The thought made me shudder, and I pushed it out of my mind.

"... we're all she has now, Peter," my mother was saying. "She needs us. We have to be patient."

Dad's tone became firm again. "Patience is one thing, but if the cost is the well-being of everyone else in the family, that's something else again. Look at us right this minute — sneaking out to the garage like a couple of thieves, just so we can have a private conversation. I feel guilty, and I don't even know why!"

Now it was my mother's turn to sigh. "Oh, Peter, I know your mother interferes, she can be cranky, she is critical, and she smokes too much. But she's your *mother*. We're just going to have to learn to live with those things."

"And what if we can't?"

"What do you mean? What other choice do we have?" And then Mom wasn't whispering any more. "No, Peter! Don't even think that."

I didn't understand. What was Mom talking about? I listened harder.

"*Shhhh*," Dad quieted her. "I know you don't like it. Do you think I do? But put your feelings aside for a moment, Tara, and be honest. It was a mistake for us to try to look after Mother ourselves. It's not working out — not for us or the kids, and not for my mother either. As much as I dislike the idea, I think we're going to have to consider a nursing home. At any rate, I'm going to make a few inquiries."

I didn't dare stay to hear any more. But as I tip-toed away, I couldn't help feeling that I'd just been granted a wish. From the sound of things, Gramma Granville was going to be moving out. And that meant I was going to get my life back.

10

.... For the rest of the day it was like a hundred butterflies had been let loose in my stomach. I felt alive again. I was going to get my room back — and my gerbils too! It was exactly what I'd been praying for. Just the same, I kept my excitement to myself. If my parents found out I'd been listening to their conversation, they would not be pleased.

But that didn't stop me from making plans. First of all, I was going to put my bedroom exactly the way it used to be. My bed, with its comfy quilt, would be back under the window, and Sandy and Sandy would be on the dresser where they belonged, gnawing on paper-towel rolls. I could see it all in my mind. When no one was looking, I hugged myself. I could hardly wait. My run of bad luck finally seemed to be coming to an end.

Then the phone rang, and I had something new to worry about.

.... I watched as the car turned out of the driveway and sped off toward my school. Then I sat down on the front steps to wait — and worry.

No other teacher had ever phoned my parents before. Why had Mr. Brockhurst? I was mortified. I was also baffled. I tried to think of what I had done that was horrible enough to prompt a phone call home. But I couldn't think of a thing.

Except maybe my grades. My marks had dropped a bit lately, but they weren't *that* bad. I was still passing everything. And anyway, it really wasn't my fault. I was doing my work. It was just that Mr. Brockhurst was marking me extra hard because he knew I didn't like him.

Of course, that's not what Mr. Brockhurst was going to tell my parents. I was pretty sure about that. What *was* he going to say? And then what were my mom and dad going to say to me?

I was still mulling over the problem when the car pulled back into the driveway. The doors banged shut with an unnerving, hollow *thunk*. But instead of heading for the house, my parents turned toward the street, and my father motioned me to follow them.

"C'mon, Annie," he said. His voice didn't give

me any hint about his mood. "Let's go for a walk."

I gulped and started down the driveway. I had no idea what was going on, but I was fairly certain I was about to find out. And from the look of my parents, I wasn't going to like it.

After half a block, nobody had said a word, and I was getting more and more nervous. Finally I couldn't stand the suspense a second longer.

"I'll work harder," I blurted. "I promise."

I don't know what reaction I had expected, but it wasn't the one I got. My mother smiled the saddest smile I've ever seen, and my dad put a hand on my shoulder and steered me left.

"Let's go to the park," he said.

I felt a wave of heat rush through my body, and then a current of cold. This was worse than I'd thought. I looked at my parents, but their faces were stony again. Finally we stopped at a bench away from the main path.

"Am I in trouble?" I asked anxiously.

My mother swallowed me up in her arms, and I was shocked at how bony she felt. "No, sweetie. You're not in trouble," she murmured into my hair. The words were reassuring, but her voice wasn't. She sounded so unhappy.

I peered up at her. "Why did Mr. Brockhurst want to see you? Was it because of my marks?"

It was my father who answered me. "Partly," he said. "But it's more than that. He is concerned about you, Annie. He thinks something's bothering you. He ..." Dad paused. "He showed us your journal."

I practically leaped off the bench. "What?! How dare he! That's supposed to be private!" Those were my personal thoughts. Mr. Brockhurst had no right!

"He said he'd noticed a difference in you from when he first came to your class as a substitute. Back then you were bouncier, he said. You smiled more, were more outgoing — generally a lot happier. At first he thought it was because you missed Mrs. Pauls, but when things didn't improve and your marks started to slide, he checked your journal to see if it might hint at what was bothering you."

"That's an invasion of privacy!" I protested again. My hatred of Mr. Brockhurst flared up once more. I'd known all along he was a horrible person, and now he'd proven it.

"He wasn't trying to pry, sweetheart," my mother said in her soothing voice. "He was trying to help."

"I don't care. He had no business ..." That was as much as I could get out. Anger was choking me, and I could feel my eyes starting to sting.

"I know it must feel that way, Annie," my dad said. "It's a shock. And you're right — the things you put in your journal are nobody's business but your own. Mr. Brockhurst knows that too. He was very apologetic."

I bet he was! At that moment, I despised Mr. Brockhurst more than ever, but I didn't say anything.

I stared at my hands and concentrated on controlling my feelings.

"If you remember that your teacher did it because he cares about you, dear, it might make you feel better," Mom said. "I believe in your right to privacy too, Annie, but I'm awfully glad Mr. Brockhurst did what he did — and that he called us. Otherwise we might never have known anything was bothering you. We *should* have noticed something was wrong. But we didn't. Things have been so crazy around home lately that we weren't paying attention. I'm sorry, Annie."

Suddenly my anger turned to guilt. As if my mother didn't have enough problems, I was making another one for her.

"Nothing's wrong," I protested. "Honest. Mr. Brockhurst doesn't know me, that's all. I'm fine." I looked at my parents to see if they were buying my story. It didn't look like they were. "Really!" I insisted. "There's not a problem."

"Annie," my mother reminded me, "we read your journal."

"But it didn't say anything!" I almost yelled.

Dad put a hand on my arm. "That's just it. Until a little while ago, your journal was full of the things you were doing and thinking and feeling. Some days you wrote several pages. Near the end of your longer entries there was one about your grandmother coming to live with us, and your concerns about that.

Then you talked about your gerbils moving to Joel's house. After that, the only thing you ever wrote was the date and the same sentence over and over — *I have nothing to say.*" He added, "Except for one other entry — *No more History Repeats Itself.*"

It could have been worse, I consoled myself. Instead of nothing, I could've written what I was actually thinking. Then I'd really have had some explaining to do. "I just got tired of writing in my journal — that's all," I insisted.

I tried to make it sound like it wasn't a big deal, but I guess I'm not a good liar. At least, my parents didn't look very convinced.

"Annie," Mom squeezed my hand, "it's okay. We're not angry with you. A lot has happened — sharing a bedroom with Claire, moving your gerbils next door. And then finding out that the club you wanted to join has disbanded. That's a lot to take. Of course, you're upset. Who wouldn't be? But you should have said something to us. It's not good to hold your feelings inside. Tell us when things are bothering you — we can help."

More than anything, I wanted to do exactly what my mother had said. But I couldn't. It wouldn't be fair. She looked so tired and worried. The last thing she needed was another problem. Besides, there wasn't anything she could do.

So I lied.

"I'm okay. At first I didn't want to share a bedroom

with Claire, but it's not that bad. And Joel is taking good care of my gerbils." At least that part was true. "I still see them every day." I didn't add, *But it's not the same.*

Mom and Dad hadn't mentioned the situation with Gramma, so I stayed far away from that topic. Soon she would be gone anyway, so what did it matter? I only had to put up with her for a little while longer.

History Repeats Itself was a different story, though. My parents knew how much it had meant to me, so there was no point pretending it hadn't.

"I was disappointed when I found out about History Repeats Itself. But there isn't anything I can do about it." Then I tried to smile. "Anyway, who knows? Maybe it'll start up again one day." I hoped I sounded more optimistic than I felt.

"Or maybe something else will come along." Mom returned my smile, and it didn't seem quite so sad this time. I had a feeling she was hinting at something.

"What do you mean?" I asked.

"Well," Dad took over, "when we explained to Mr. Brockhurst how much you'd been looking forward to joining History Repeats Itself, he told us about another activity you might enjoy instead."

I could feel my back stiffen. I wasn't interested in any suggestions that came from Mr. Brockhurst. I shook my head.

"Just listen," my father said. "Don't make up your

mind before you've even heard what it is. You might like it."

But I was determined. "Nothing could be as good as History Repeats Itself. If I can't join that, I don't want anything."

"Now you sound like Gramma," my father snapped.

That shook me out of my stubbornness in a hurry. Gramma Granville was the last person in the world I wanted to be compared to.

"Sorry," I mumbled, trying to keep the bad mood out of my voice. "What is this other — *activity*?"

"It's called the Junior Genealogical Society."

"What's that?" Not that I cared, but I felt like I should say something. I didn't want my father to bark at me again.

"It's an organization — a club — for young people like you, and what it does is teach you how to trace your family tree. You learn different ways of finding out about your family's past. Some people have traced their ancestors back hundreds of years. And you'd be amazed at the number of connections they find to famous historical figures like kings and queens, politicians, and even outlaws."

That sounded sort of interesting. Then I remembered it was Mr. Brockhurst's suggestion, and I hardened my heart again.

"What do you think?" my mother asked hopefully.

"It's not History Repeats Itself," I grumbled.

"No, it's not." Dad's tone was brittle.

"But it can't hurt to give it a try, can it?" There was Mom's cheery voice again. Without looking, I could see the bluish hollows beneath her eyes and the weary smile on her mouth. Even sick, she kept trying to please everyone. I didn't have the heart to disappoint her — but that didn't mean I had to like it.

"Fine," I frowned. "I'll try it."

11

.... The next meeting of the Junior Genealogical Society was Saturday morning. It still bugged me that it was Mr. Brockhurst's idea, but there wasn't much I could do about that. Of course, Joel thought it was the greatest thing he'd ever heard of — Joel has no sense of loyalty. Just the same, when he volunteered to come along, I didn't say no.

So Saturday morning my father dropped us off at an antique shop on Fort Street, where the meetings were held.

He seemed to sense that I was a bit uneasy. "I checked the place out when I registered you guys the other day," he said. "Inside the front door, there's a staircase on your left. You can't miss it. There's a sign there too. Take those stairs. The meeting room is at the top."

I filed his instructions into my brain.

"Look." Dad nodded toward the sidewalk. "There's a boy about your age heading inside right now. I bet he's going to the same place you are. Why don't you follow him?"

He checked his watch. "It's almost ten o'clock. I have to be at the golf course in twenty minutes. You'll be done before I'm finished golfing, so Joel's dad is going to pick you up. He'll meet you here in two hours."

Joel and I let ourselves out of the car. "Have fun." Dad waved and grinned, and then he was gone.

Joel took a deep breath, and I wondered if he was nervous too. "Well, here goes nothing," he said, yanking open the shop door. "But I'm tellin' ya, Annie, if I find out I had a great-great-great grandfather wanted for murder or something, I'm blaming it all on you."

I followed him through the door. "What if you find out he was a rich prince?"

Joel grinned over his shoulder. "Then I'm claiming the money, of course."

Walking inside the antique store was like entering another world. The whoosh of traffic and the clopping of feet disappeared as soon as we closed the door, and a spooky quiet took over, as if the plush red carpet and heavy embroidered tapestries were absorbing every sound. It was like being inside a museum. An elegant lady with bleached white hair and an armful of silver bracelets turned from the candlesticks she was examining and frowned at us over the top of her half-glasses. We got the message and clamped our mouths shut.

Just as Dad had said, the Junior Genealogical Society was at the top of the stairs. The door was open, so we walked in. The room was a cross between a classroom and a library, and unlike the depressingly dark stairwell, it was bright. Sunlight flooded through a large leaded glass window and bounced off white plastered walls that were lined with shelves of books, rolled papers, maps, stacks of pictures, and lots of other stuff I didn't recognize. A couple of computers were set up in a corner, and round tables surrounded by metal chairs filled the rest of the room.

Some of the chairs were already occupied, and a couple of kids looked up when we came in. Joel shuffled his feet. He was obviously as uncomfortable as I was.

"Sit anywhere," said a thin boy with dishwater-colored hair and eyes. "Gordon will be here in a couple of minutes." Then he went back to the collection of books and papers spread out in front of him.

We slithered into chairs at the nearest vacant table.

"Who's Gordon?" Joel hissed.

"I don't know. Maybe he's in charge."

Joel looked around the room and began drumming his fingers on the table — until I poked him in the ribs with my elbow. After a while another boy and girl arrived and sat down with the thin boy who'd spoken to us. A few minutes after that a girl came in, dropped her backpack onto a chair and wandered over to the shelves.

"I think we're the only rookies," Joel said.

I nodded.

"I wish this Gordon guy would hurry up."

As if on cue, voices floated up through the stairwell.

"I bet that's him now," I whispered.

Then there was a thunderous laugh, and Joel quipped, "Either that or the Jolly Green Giant."

The owner of the laugh really was a giant. A huge man — both tall and wide — Gordon Macmillan had the merriest face I'd ever seen. His blue eyes sparkled nonstop and, as Joel and I soon discovered, even when he was serious, his face seemed to be on the verge of a smile. The second I saw him, my nervousness melted away.

Joel had been right — he and I were the only new members of the group. After a bunch of questions for Gordon, the other kids got down to work, and a kind of hum settled over the room.

Gordon lowered himself onto a chair at our table. For a second I worried the chair was going to break, but it just groaned a little. Gordon smiled his huge smile, and we smiled back. Everything about Gordon was big, and his voice boomed as he said,

"So, you want to become JGS detectives, do you?"

Joel and I exchanged puzzled looks.

"What's a JGS detective?" Joel asked. "I thought we were gonna find out about our ancestors." His eyes darted around the room. "Are we in the right place?"

Gordon's smile turned into a deep, rumbling chuckle. "JGS stands for Junior Genealogical Society," he explained. "Sounds pretty boring, eh? I prefer to think of us as detectives, and this place as our detective agency. We gather clues and try to figure out what they mean. It's a lot like putting together a jigsaw puzzle. The only difference is you have to find the pieces yourself, *and* you don't know what the puzzle is supposed to look like until it's finished." He grinned, and then sobered once more. "It's not for everybody, though. Hunting for clues is hard work." Then the grin was back. "But it's also a lot of fun, and when you find a piece that fits the puzzle, it's one of the most exhilarating feelings there is. It's like you're bringing the past to life again."

I perked up. That was exactly how I'd felt about History Repeats Itself. Was it possible that JGS could be the same? I liked Gordon, and what he'd said so far was interesting. It got me thinking, and I asked, "But how do you know what to look for? And how do you know when you've found it?"

"*Ahh*," Gordon winked. "There are hundreds of ways. Old letters, history books, birth and death certificates, maps, photographs, gazetteers, the Web —"

he took a breath and spread his arms to take in the room "— the sources are practically endless." Then he pushed himself away from the table. "Come on. I'll give you a tour of the place and get you started."

The more Gordon showed us and told us, the more excited Joel and I became, and before we knew it, it was time to leave. In fact, Mr. Werner was already waiting when we got back to the street.

"You're fifteen minutes late." He tapped his watch. "I thought I was going to have to come looking for you."

"Hey, Dad, you should see this place," Joel started in even before we'd shut the van door. "We've learned piles of stuff already. It's so neat, I can hardly wait to go back. Gordon — he's the guy who runs everything — he's pretty cool, and *really* smart. He spent practically the whole time with Annie and me. He showed us how to use atlases and almanacs and history books to find out things about our families. And on the computer — you're not gonna believe this!" Joel was bubbling like a soft drink. "He found our surnames — that's what you call last names in genealogy talk — and it turns out Annie and me might even be related! Can you believe it?"

"What are you talking about?" Mr. Werner was trying to listen and drive at the same time.

"Well, Gordon hunted down Granville on the computer all the way to a family in Ontario that's already traced a bunch of people in their family tree, and back in the 1800s, there was a Bernhardt Werner in their family. Isn't that unbelievable? If Annie is related to that Granville, and if I'm related to that Werner, then we might be related to each other!" Joel finally had to stop because he'd run out of breath.

"That's a lot of '*ifs*'," Mr. Werner chuckled. "How do you find out for sure?"

"Well," I took over, "the first thing we have to do is make a list of our relatives as far back as we can, and write down everything we know about them — like when they were born and died, the jobs they did, where they lived — that kind of thing. That's our assignment for next Saturday."

"It's like a treasure hunt," Joel beamed.

"A treasure hunt?" Mr. Werner looked puzzled.

I shook my head and made a face at Joel. "Your son thinks he's going to discover he's inherited a pile of money."

"You never know," Joel said. "Remember all the things Gordon said he's found out about *his* ancestors. He had a great-great-great-great-great somebody who —"

"Uncle," I said.

"Whatever." Joel seemed unconcerned. "He was related to Gordon somehow, and he was an officer in Napoleon's army! If he can be related to somebody like that, I don't see why I can't —" His argument was cut short by the wailing of a siren. Mr. Werner glanced in his rear-view mirror and then pulled over to the side of the road. A fire truck with its lights flashing whizzed past.

"I wonder where it's going," I said.

It turned left at the next intersection. We turned left too. The fire engine was already speeding ahead, but we followed it for several blocks. Then it turned left again.

"Hey, that's our street!" Joel exclaimed.

He was right. I craned my neck to see what was burning. But as we turned the corner, my curiosity turned to horror, and my stomach dropped into my shoes.

The fire was at *my* house!

12

.... The fire truck was blocking
the Werners' driveway as well as ours, so Joel's dad
had to drive further down the street. I was practically clawing at the window, trying to spot someone
in my family. But all I could see were firefighters and
miles of hose.

We were getting further and further away, and
Mr. Werner still hadn't found a place to park. Why
didn't he just stop the car? Didn't he know I had to
get out?

Finally he pulled up to the curb, and I shot out
the door, back toward my house. Joel's dad yelled
something at me, but I didn't hear. I pushed past the
gawking neighbors lining the sidewalks. As I darted
anxiously through the confusion, my heart pounded
in my ears. The front door of the house was wide
open, and the air smelled of smoke, but there was

no sign of my family — anywhere! I began to panic. Where were they?

I tripped over an enormous gray hose.

"Keep the area clear, folks." A firefighter in a fluorescent yellow jacket stopped me from falling, but also kept me from going any further.

I tried to squirm out of his grasp. "Let me go! This is my house!"

That didn't make any difference to him, though. Finally Joel and his dad arrived to free me. Then Mr. Werner began asking questions.

"What happened? Is anyone hurt? How bad is it?"

I didn't stick around to hear the answers. I had spotted my mother in front of the garage with another firefighter, and I tore off toward her.

"Mom! Mom!" I screamed, practically throwing myself at her. "Are you okay?"

"I'm fine, Annie." Mom gave me a squeeze. "Don't worry. No one is hurt. It looks much worse than it is. I'll explain as soon as I've answered a few questions for this fireman."

But I wasn't about to let her go.

Joel and his dad had once again caught up to me, and when Mom saw them, she said, "Thanks for bringing Annie home, Steve." Then she gestured to the confusion around us. "As you can see, things are a bit muddled at the moment. Shelly took Fiona to your house. This fire business has really upset her —

poor thing. I'll come and fetch her in a few minutes, but I have to take care of things here first. Could I ask you to keep Annie at your place too until I'm finished?"

I pulled back and opened my mouth to protest, but my mother's raised finger stopped me.

"Are you sure I can't help out here?" Mr. Werner asked.

My mom shook her head and turned to me. For someone who was sick, she was pretty bossy. "I want you to stay at Joel's house. Do you understand me, Annie? It's a zoo here, and I don't want you mixed up in it. Make sure Gramma is all right. I'll be there in a little while."

"What about Dad and Claire?" I asked.

"Your father is still golfing, and Claire is at the mall. Gramma and I were the only ones home."

"Are you sure you're all right?" Mr. Werner asked, concern lining his face. "I could come back after I drop the kids off."

Mom shook her head. "No. Thanks anyway, but there really isn't anything you can do. And I won't be long."

When we got to Joel's house, my grandmother was sleeping. We quizzed Mrs. Werner about the fire, but she didn't seem to know any more than we did. So, as much as I didn't like it, I had no choice but to wait for my mom.

I sat glued to the window, imagining a hundred

different ways the fire might have started. But no matter how it had begun, there was one thing I was sure of — it had been my grandmother's fault. Most likely, she'd dropped another lighted match — one that hadn't gone out. Or maybe she'd fallen asleep while she was smoking. Gramma was very careless. She might have forgotten she'd even lit a cigarette and just left it. It could have fallen out of the ashtray and started the fire that way.

And what if someone *had* been hurt? I pictured my mother standing in front of the garage, and I cringed. The house could have burned to the ground — and my mother with it! Once again anger welled up inside me, and I prayed that my father had made the inquiries he'd talked about. Things were becoming impossible. It wasn't any longer just that my grandmother was a miserable old woman who'd turned my life upside down — she was actually dangerous!

13

.... As it turned out, there hadn't been a fire at all — just a lot of smoke. And though I was right about Gramma causing it, a cigarette hadn't been the culprit.

It had been a cooking accident. With Dad, Claire, and I away, and Mom asleep, my grandmother had decided to make her own lunch — soup. But after she'd put the pot on the stove, she'd forgotten about it and dozed off. Eventually the soup had boiled away, scorching the pan and sending up horrid-smelling smoke that set off the alarm. Startled awake, Mom had rushed out of her bedroom into the smoke-filled hallway. Thinking smoke meant fire, she'd dialed 911 and then hurried Gramma out of the house.

The firefighters had been pretty understanding, though. This obviously wasn't the first time they'd been called to a "not-quite" fire, and while it was a relief, we were all shaken up, especially Gramma. She was completely flustered and kept saying the same things over and over — stuff that didn't make any sense. The part I couldn't believe, though, was the way she lied. She flat out denied having anything to do with the fire. In fact, she accused my mother of starting it!

There was no way I was going to let her get away with that. But when I went to stick up for my mom, she shushed me. Well, she didn't exactly tell me to be quiet, but she gave me her *don't say anything* look. I couldn't believe it. Gramma had accused her of a crime *she'd* committed herself, yet my mother was protecting her. Why? It didn't make sense — and it wasn't right!

There was one good thing that happened because of the fire, though. My grandmother spent the night at Joel's house. The grownups decided she would be more comfortable in the Werners' guest room than at our house. As for Mom and Dad and Claire and me, we went home and threw open all the doors and windows to clear away the smoky smell, then ordered a pizza and ate it in the backyard.

Since my grandmother had arrived, this was the first time my family had felt like it was supposed to. It was as if Gramma had become a huge weight we carried around all the time. Now suddenly that weight had been lifted, and we were lounging on lawn chairs in the backyard, wolfing down pizza, guzzling soft drinks — and laughing. Even my mother looked less stressed out. That was pretty amazing, considering the scare we'd just had. But as far as I was concerned, it was worth it. I didn't care that the house reeked of smoke. I was just glad to have my family back.

I helped myself to a third slice of pepperoni pizza.

Dad tossed his napkin into the nearly empty box and said, "Considering today's catastrophe, I don't know why I feel so good. But I do." For a second I wondered if he'd been reading my mind.

"It's probably the five pieces of pizza you scarfed down," Claire teased.

Dad leaned back and hooked his hands behind his head. "Never mind. I'm a growing boy," he grinned.

"Yes, and we know exactly where you're grow-ing." My mother laughed and poked Dad's stomach.

"You know," Claire said, "I think this is the first pizza we've had since Gramma's come to live with us."

It was true, but I wished Claire hadn't mentioned Gramma. Tonight she was at Joel's house, and I wanted her to stay there.

Dad lowered his arms and cleared his throat. "Actually, that's something I need to talk to you all about."

"Having pizza more often?" Claire grinned.

"No," Dad smiled back. "Your grandmother."

Thud! She was back.

"Your mother and I have been talking about how

things have changed since Gramma moved in. It's been a tough adjustment for everyone, including her. And I'm not sure — especially in light of what happened today — that we can continue with things as they are."

"I don't get what you're saying," Claire frowned.

I thought I did, but I wasn't supposed to know anything about this, so I kept quiet.

There was a pause as Dad seemed to be organizing his thoughts.

Finally he said, "Today's fire —"

"It was just smoke," Claire corrected him.

Dad nodded. "True. It was. But it very easily could have become a fire. The point is, your grandmother needs more attention than we can give her."

"It was an accident!" Claire objected.

Dad sighed heavily. I could tell this wasn't easy for him.

"Yes, Claire, it was. But how long until there's another accident — maybe one more serious? We can't take that chance."

"What are you saying?" Claire's eyes darted back and forth between my parents. Then they narrowed suspiciously, and she said, "You want to put Gramma in an old folks' home, don't you?"

My father stiffened. "Let's get one thing straight," he said. "I don't *want* to put Gramma anywhere." Then his whole body went slack. "But I'm not sure we have a choice."

"Of course we have a choice!" It was Claire again. "Gramma can keep on living with *us*. You can't put her in one of those places. It'd be like — throwing her away!"

My father actually went white. It was my mother who answered.

"Think about what you're saying, Claire."

"I am!" she snapped. "You're the ones who aren't thinking. So Gramma's a little forgetful. So she needs a cane. So what? She's family! Doesn't that count for anything?"

Claire paused long enough to scowl at Mom and Dad and take another breath, but not long enough to let them answer. When she started up again, she was waving her arms.

"Gramma's the one who taught me how to swim. She made clothes for all my dolls. I stayed with her for three whole summers of my life! Am I just supposed to forget all that because she's old?"

"Of course not," my mother said quietly. "Try to understand, Claire. This is not an easy decision. We don't want to do this."

"Then why are you?" Claire demanded.

"Gramma's health and safety, for one thing," Dad said. "And there's your mother to consider too."

"What do you mean?"

"I mean your mother isn't well enough to look after Gramma by herself all day while we're not home."

"Then why don't we hire somebody? A live-in nurse would be way cheaper than a nursing home anyway."

My father shook his head. "Where would we put a nurse? We have no room for another body. We're tripping over one another as it is."

Then suddenly Claire had tears in her eyes. I was surprised. Claire yelled a lot, but she almost never cried. "Please, Dad, don't do this!" she pleaded. "I don't want Gramma to go to one of those places. She should be with us. I love her."

Dad looked straight at Claire. It was easy to tell he wasn't happy. "I love her too," he said quietly, "but I don't know what else to do."

There was a very long silence.

At last, Dad started talking again. "I've put applications in at a couple of different nursing homes. But until there's an opening, we're going to have to make the best of things here."

"How long will that be?" Mom asked.

"It's hard to say," Dad sighed. "But they tell me the wait can be as much as two years."

Suddenly I wasn't hungry any more, and the piece of pizza I'd been eating slid onto the grass.

14

.... It looked like I was right
back where I'd started, except I felt worse than ever
— not just because Gramma wasn't going to be moving out for a long time, but because it seemed like I
was the only one who wanted her to. And that made
me wonder if there was something wrong with *me*.

Why was I the only one who wanted her to leave?
When I'd overheard my parents in the garage, I had
been sure my father felt the same way I did, but he'd
told Claire that he didn't want Gramma to go. As for
my mother, she should have been happier than anyone to get rid of Gramma, yet she'd been against the
idea of a nursing home from the very beginning. Even
Claire wanted Gramma to stay.

Maybe I could have accepted my family's attitude
if I had at least liked my grandmother — but I *didn't*.
What was there to like? She didn't do anything but sit

and smoke. She wasn't fun. She didn't laugh. She didn't even smile! The only time she opened her mouth was to eat and complain.

But none of that mattered. My grandmother was going to be with us for a long time whether I liked it or not and — unless *I* moved out — I was going to have to learn to live with the situation.

I decided the best thing was to stay out of my grandmother's way. To begin with, I could ask Claire to trade chores with me — the bathroom for the living room. *Ugh!* The thought of cleaning the toilet was disgusting, but it was still better than having Gramma tell me how to vacuum and point out all the places I missed with the dust cloth. The rest of the time, I could hang out at Joel's house. Except for chores and meals, I was pretty much doing that anyway.

I wouldn't be able to avoid my grandmother completely, but if I could keep a distance between us most of the time, I might be able to survive.

Part of the problem, though, was that Gramma was on my mind almost all the time. What I needed was something else to think about. I was hoping the Junior Genealogical Society might be that something. Even so, I didn't start working on the assignment Gordon had given us until Wednesday night after supper.

I dragged the family Bible out of the bookcase and plunked it down on the kitchen table beside my pencils and a thick pad of yellow newsprint. Then I printed my name neatly at the top of the pad — Ann Elizabeth Granville. There. I was ready to begin.

The Bible had been passed down to my mother from her father, who had received it from his father before that. I didn't know how many other people it had belonged to, but it was very old. It had loose photographs and papers stuffed inside, and I was tempted to poke through them, but then I remembered what Gordon had said about the importance of being methodical, so I flipped through the old leather book in search of some sort of family record instead.

I found it on the inside back page. It had no title, but I knew right away that it was what I was looking for. The handwriting and ink changed several times — it was a pretty scruffy-looking document, but when I saw it, I felt as if I'd discovered gold. To someone else, it would have been nothing more than a list of names with dates noted in brackets, but to me, it was the first piece of my family puzzle.

I scanned the page. The first entry was Joshua Stephen Michael Cooper (b. 1883 d. 1943). That must have been my great-great-great grandfather. I felt a shiver shoot up my spine. Gordon was right — uncovering the past *was* exciting.

My eyes jumped down to the bottom of the page. I recognized my mother's handwriting even before I read what she'd written. Dad's name was entered beside hers with their wedding date and Dad's birthday. Claire's name came after that, and then there was mine. It felt weird to see myself on the same page with someone who'd been born over a hundred years before.

On the yellow pad, I drew two short lines from my name. Below one I wrote my father's name. Below the other I wrote my mother's. Then I drew lines down from my mom's name and entered the names of the other people recorded in the Bible.

I looked at what I had so far. There were lots of gaps — unknown husbands and wives, mostly — but I was confident I could find the missing pieces in the photographs and scraps of paper scattered throughout the pages of the Bible.

I turned to my father's branch of the tree. Beside his name, I wrote Mark Brian Granville m. Margaret — then I stopped. I didn't know Aunt Meg's middle name or even what her last name had been before she married Uncle Mark. Oh well, I was pretty sure my parents could help me out there. Then I drew a line down from Dad's name and wrote in Gramma and Grandpa Granville. I didn't know their middle names either. I didn't even have any idea when they'd been born or when Grandpa Tom had died.

I put my pencil down. I had reached my first roadblock. Mom was napping and my father was working late, so I wouldn't be able to fill in any of the missing information until later, unless ... For a split second I considered asking my grandmother for help, but just as quickly, I rejected the idea. All she would do was growl at me. I sighed and turned back to the Bible. I would look through the pictures and papers inside instead.

Then I heard the *thump, thump, thump* of my grandmother's cane, and I glanced up.

"Don't look so startled," she frowned. "I'm not going to bite you. I just want a cup of tea."

"I'll get it for you, Gramma," I said, jumping up.

She waved her cane at me and scowled harder — if that was possible. "I'm not an invalid, you know," she said. "I'm surprised you people let me blow my own nose. I'm perfectly capable of making a pot of tea, thank you." And then she waved her cane at me again. "Sit down and get on with whatever you were doing."

I tried, but it was hard to concentrate with my grandmother just a couple of steps away. I felt guilty. I should have thought about asking her if she needed anything. My mother wouldn't like it if she knew Gramma was having to fend for herself.

She filled the kettle and plugged it in. Then she dumped the old tea out of the pot and rinsed it. When the kettle started to boil, she poured a small amount of water from it into the teapot and sloshed it around. Then she dumped that out too. Finally, she put a fresh tea bag into the pot and poured boiling water over it.

As she clinked the lid into place, I asked, "Why did you rinse the teapot twice?"

"Hmmph?" She looked up. "What are you talking about?"

"The teapot — first you rinsed it with tap water, and then you rinsed it again with boiling water from the kettle. Why?"

She gave her head a shake, as if I had just asked the most stupid question ever. "Because that's how you make tea."

"That's not how I make tea," I said.

"Then you're not doing it properly," she shrugged, and tugged on the cupboard door above her.

I opened my mouth to protest, but then closed it again. *No* — I wasn't going to let her make me mad.

Gramma shut the cupboard and opened the one next to it. Then she muttered something I didn't catch and closed that door too.

"Where does your mother keep her cups and saucers?" she snapped.

I pointed to a cupboard across the kitchen. "Would you like me to get you one?"

Gramma scowled. "Why would she keep them way over there? It makes more sense to have them here."

"Would you like me to get you one?" I asked again, trying to ignore the criticism.

"Fine," she grumbled, and as I pushed myself up from the table, she added, "You might as well get yourself one too."

That surprised me, but I didn't say anything. I put the cups and saucers on the counter, and then went to the fridge for milk. Gramma had the tea poured by the time I came back.

"Sugar?" She sounded impatient, as if I should have volunteered the information without being asked.

"Yes, please," I said quickly. I poured the milk. "Would you like me to carry your tea into the living room, Gramma?"

Wagging a hand toward the kitchen table where I was working, she said, "Put it down there."

"Oh," I blurted stupidly. I hadn't expected her to have her tea with me. And I had to admit that I wasn't overjoyed at the idea either. However, I couldn't very well say that, so I put our cups on the table and pulled out a chair for my grandmother. Then I slid back into my own place.

Gramma lifted her cup to her mouth and after blowing on it for a few seconds lowered it back to the saucer. "Schoolwork?" she barked, nodding at the papers strewn around me.

I shook my head. "No. This is for that genealogy club I joined."

Gramma pulled the yellow pad toward her. She looked at it for a few seconds and then said, "Thomas Peter Granville."

"Pardon?"

She stabbed at the pad with her finger. "Thomas Peter Granville — that was your grandfather's full name. You'll be wanting that, I presume. He was born on July 19, 1912 in Ottawa. Died on November 7, 1979."

Then she pushed the pad back toward me.

I grabbed my pencil and scribbled in the information. I could feel her eyes on me. When I'd finished, she barked, "Fiona Ethel Catherine Humboldt — that was my maiden name. I imagine you'll need that for your chart too. The Ethel was for my mother, the Catherine for her mother. The Fiona was just because my parents liked it." Then she snorted. "There's no accounting for taste."

When I'd finished adding Gramma's full name to my family tree, she said, "What else do you need to know?"

I looked at my chart and then at my grandmother. "Anything," I shrugged. "Everything. What about your parents and brothers and sisters? Do you remember their birthdays and stuff?"

My grandmother snorted again. "What do you take me for?" she demanded. "I may not always remember what day it is or where I've left my cane, but I'm not about to forget my own family."

Gramma talked way faster than I could write, and several times I had to ask her to slow down. She grumbled at me for not keeping up, but she did repeat the information. An hour later, I had filled several pages of my yellow pad, and yet I had the feeling that I had barely begun to tap my grandmother's storehouse of knowledge.

I hadn't drunk any of my tea either. I peered across the table at Gramma's cup. It was still full too.

15

.... On Saturday morning Joel
and I were back at the JGS Detective Agency.

"Holy cow!" Joel exclaimed, eyeing my stack of
notes. "How'd you get so much information?" He
poked through my papers, and then his eyes narrowed
suspiciously. "You made this stuff up, didn't you?"

I punched him in the arm. "I did not. Don't be
dumb." Then I put on my snobbiest face. "I'm just a
good researcher."

"No, seriously," Joel insisted. "Has somebody else
in your family already done a family tree?"

I shook my head.

"Then how'd you find out so much?"

"Most of the stuff about my mom's side of the
family was in an old Bible. And the information about
my dad's side, I got from my grandmother."

Joel's eyebrows shot up. "Really? That's a surprise.

I would've bet a year's allowance you'd have bitten off your tongue and swallowed it before you'd have asked your grandmother *anything*."

Joel was right, but it sounded horrible to hear him say it.

"Actually, I didn't ask her," I confessed. "She just kind of poked into what I was doing the other night and started telling me stuff."

"Cool," Joel said. "Maybe I should give *my* granny a call." Then he grinned. "If my parents will pay the long-distance charges, that is. You're lucky," he added, turning to his own notes. "Your grandmother is right in your house. You can ask her anything whenever you want."

I didn't know if I agreed with Joel about being lucky. But he was right about Gramma being a good source of family history. In just one hour she'd told me more about my relatives than I had learned during the whole rest of my life. And for some reason, that made me think about her differently than I had before. It wasn't as if I suddenly thought she was a wonderful person or anything like that. Even when she'd been helping me with my family tree, she'd been as grouchy as ever.

But I did feel something — surprise, maybe? Or respect? I couldn't quite put my finger on it. It was sort of the way you might feel if you discovered Clark Kent was Superman. I'm not saying I was starting to see my grandmother as a super-hero, but I was beginning to realize there was more to her than I'd thought.

And I was curious to discover what that was. Nevertheless, I pushed my curiosity to the back of my mind. The chances of Gramma telling me anything more were almost non-existent. The other night had been a fluke. For some reason, she'd had a weak moment. But she was past it now. If anything, she'd been grumpier than ever the last few days. If I wanted to find the missing pieces of my family's history, I was going to have to search somewhere else.

And the first place I was going to look was in our family's heirlooms, because that was the assignment Gordon had given us for the next week. Heirlooms, he said, could be just about anything — jewelry, china, clothes, books, silver — it didn't matter as long as they had been passed down through the family.

I started my search at the lunch table as soon as I got home.

"Where'd we get these dishes?" I asked my mom as I reached for a second ham sandwich.

"Eaton's, I think," she said.

I studied my soup spoon critically for a few seconds and then turned to her again. "And the silverware? Where'd that come from?"

"It was a wedding gift."

My parents had been married nearly twenty years, so that meant the silverware was getting old — but that still didn't make it an heirloom.

"What about that vase?" I pointed to the center-piece, a small vase with an Oriental scene painted on it.

"Uncle Mark and Aunt Meg brought that back from China a few years ago." My mother looked at me curiously. "What's with the third degree? Are you taking inventory for insurance purposes or something?"

"No," I giggled, and then explained the assignment.

My mother nodded. "I see. Well, I'm sure we must have a few heirlooms kicking around somewhere."

"I've got some underwear that used to belong to my brother," Dad offered. "Would you like to have a look at that?"

"That's gross," Claire groaned.

"Hardly appropriate mealtime conversation," Gramma muttered.

Dad pretended his feelings were hurt. "Fine," he sniffed. "I was only trying to help."

My mother smiled. "Never mind, dear," she said. "Eat your soup."

.... After lunch, I went next door to check on my gerbils, but I didn't stay. Joel was at a baseball game, and it felt weird hanging out at his house when he wasn't there.

"Your grandmother has been looking for you," Mom said the second I walked back in the door.

I stopped. What had I done wrong? "Why?" I asked warily.

Mom closed the book she was reading and looked up. She smiled. "Perhaps you should ask her. She's in her bedroom."

As I headed down the hall, I began wishing I'd stayed at Joel's house. But it was too late now. Gramma's door was closed. With a little luck, she would be sleeping. I tapped lightly.

"Who's there?"

So much for luck.

"It's Annie, Gramma. Mom said you wanted to see me."

"Well, open the door so I can," she barked back.

It was sort of eerie letting myself into my old room. I hadn't been in it since Gramma had moved in, and that was nearly three months ago. Now it was a totally different place — not just the way it was decorated, but the way it felt and smelled too. There was nothing of me left there. It was almost as if I'd never even been in it before. I guess that should have made me sad, but it only surprised me.

My grandmother was sitting on the chair near the little table. On the floor beside her was a brown metal steamer trunk. It had arrived by moving van with the rest of her things and had been packed away in the basement. At least, I thought it had.

"Don't just stand there," Gramma scolded me. "Sit down." Then she turned back to what looked like a jewelry box in her lap.

Since she had the only chair in the room — and I

didn't think I should sit on her bed — I lowered myself onto the carpet at her feet. Gramma's full attention was on the box. In an effort to look inside, I stretched my eyeballs as far as I could without actually moving my body, but it was impossible to see past the raised lid. The steamer trunk, on the other hand, was right beside me and wide open. Nevertheless, I resisted peeking inside. That would only get me yelled at.

There was nothing to do but wait for Gramma to get around to me. I started counting the freckles on my arm. I was up to 137 before she finally noticed me.

"Ann Elizabeth!" She said it as though I'd sneaked up on her. "What are you doing here?" Obviously, she'd forgotten this visit was her idea.

"Mom said you wanted to see me," I reminded her.

"She did?"

I nodded.

Gramma frowned. "Why would she say that?"

I started to get up. I knew from experience that arguing with my grandmother wasn't going to make her remember.

But something did, because she stopped me before I got to the door.

"What about these heirlooms?" She scowled. "Aren't you interested in them any more? Your father nearly broke his back hauling this trunk up from the basement."

16

.... It was as if Gramma had known I was going to be looking for heirlooms one day, because she had lots of them — all neatly stored in her old steamer trunk. The trunk itself was an heirloom, dating back to the early 1900s, and as Gramma pointed to the colorful stickers pasted all over the outside of it, she explained who had taken a trip where, and when, and what they'd done during it.

That struck me as pretty amazing. Gramma could remember the teeny-tiniest details about events that had taken place seventy-five years ago, but she couldn't remember what she'd had for lunch that day — or if she'd even *had* lunch. The names and birthdays and life stories of everyone from her fifth cousin nine times removed to the old man who'd lived down the street when she was a little girl were as clear in her mind as they'd ever been. Yet she could ask me the same question three times in five minutes and still forget the answer.

When I'd asked my mother why that was, she said it had to do with long- and short-term memory. She said people's brains shrank as they got older, and that affected their ability to concentrate and learn new things. It was even worse if they didn't exercise their minds by reading and solving puzzles and other stuff like that.

Considering Gramma could sit for hours doing nothing but smoking and staring out the window, I was pretty sure her brain must have shrunk big time — except the part that remembered what had happened a long time ago. That part was fine.

It was sort of spooky watching her slip into a memory. She'd pick something up and *zap!* — she'd be transported to another time. My head was spinning before we were even halfway through the trunk. Gramma had told me about so many different people and events, there was no way I could keep them all straight. Not that it mattered to Gramma. Even though she was talking to me, I had the feeling her memories were more real than I was.

I didn't mind, though, because her stories were interesting — and so was her trunk. Of all the things inside it, my favorites were the miniature portrait and the letter. They were mysterious, because they were the only things Gramma didn't know much about.

I stared at the oval of white porcelain in the palm

of my hand. The face of a young woman stared back. She was more unusual than pretty, with a tiny heart-shaped face beneath fiery copper hair. Even pulling it back into a severe bun hadn't toned it down. In contrast, the woman's round eyes were as dull as a winter sky — and just as cold. And her small, pink mouth was pinched shut as if she'd sucked on a lemon.

"Who was she?" I asked.

Gramma shook her head. "Don't know that."

"When did she live?"

"Don't know that either."

"How do you know she's a relative then?"

"I don't." Gramma shrugged. "Not for sure. But why else would her painting have been kept in the family? You're the one studying genealogy, my girl. You figure it out." Then Gramma dipped back into the trunk and pulled out a picture frame. "As I recall, the miniature and this letter here —" she offered the picture frame to me — "... are supposed to be connected in some way. I don't know how, but ..." Her shoulders hunched again.

I traded Gramma the miniature for the framed letter. It looked very old. The paper was badly yellowed, and a corner of it was missing. Even though it was protected beneath glass now, it had obviously been folded and unfolded many times, so that the words scrawled across the disintegrating creases were completely worn away.

I began reading, but it was slow going. For one

thing, the sentences were all chopped up by the words lost in the fold lines. The faded ink didn't help matters either. Neither did the handwriting with its fancy loops and tails. And then there was the grammar. Not only did the sentences sound awkward, lots of the words were misspelled, and others were capitalized in the middle of sentences for no reason at all.

The one thing that could have been a clue was the date. Unfortunately, November 15 was the only part of it that was left. The year had disappeared with the torn corner.

The letter was written by a man named William to a lady called Constance. I got the impression they were married or engaged, but that they'd been apart for quite a while. By the sounds of it, though, their separation was about to end, because William wrote that he'd find a way to bring Constance to him in the spring once the crops were planted.

I handed the frame back to my grandmother.

"So how are the letter and the miniature connected?" I asked.

"Hmmph?" Gramma was already digging into the trunk again.

I repeated my question.

"Don't ask me," she said. "All I know is that they are."

"Aren't you even a little bit curious?" I said. My mind was so full of questions, I could hardly sit still. "If William and Constance were our ancestors, I want to know about them." I began thinking out loud. "Maybe they were star-crossed lovers like Romeo and Juliet. They obviously loved each other, so why weren't they together? Do you think William could have been a criminal? And where was he? It sounds like he was on a farm, but where? What about Constance? Where was she? And how long ago did all of this happen?"

But my grandmother wasn't listening. Her attention was on a dilapidated leather eyeglass case containing a pair of wire-rimmed spectacles.

"These belonged to my father," she said. "Your great-grandfather. He was a printer, you know — one of the finest in all of Canada. He did beautiful work. Everyone said so. He even received a letter of commendation from the prime minister once. I can see it yet — my father's full name in black calligraphy and the official government seal at the bottom. I even remember how it was worded. To George Richard Humboldt, in recognition of ..." And she was off again, lost in her own world.

.... As soon as I left my grandmother, I raced for my yellow pad and began scribbling down the things she had told me. But my head was swimming with names and dates and places, and I kept getting the stories all tangled up.

I let out a huge, frustrated sigh and tossed my pencil onto the table just as my dad came into the kitchen.

"What's the problem, duck?" he asked on his way to the fridge. "The old family tree suffering from root rot?"

I shook my head. "It's not that. There are *too many* roots. I just spent the last two hours with Gramma and her trunk."

Dad winced and grabbed his back. "Ooh, yeah. That trunk."

"Gramma must have told me fifty stories about the family, but now I can't remember them."

Dad laughed. And then he said, "I'm sorry, Annie. It's just that you'd have to have a mind like a tape recorder to remember all Gramma's stories. I've been listening to them my whole life, and I still can't keep them straight. Beats me how she does it."

I cheered up. Though he didn't realize it, my father had given me an idea.

"Do you think Gramma would tell me the stories again?" I asked.

He looked sideways at me. "Is water wet?"

.... The very next day I gathered my courage and approached my grandmother with my request. Of course, she scowled at me. I had expected that. And she scolded me for not paying attention. That was no surprise either. I *had* paid attention, but I resisted the urge to tell her so.

My mother says you can catch more flies with

honey than you can with vinegar, so instead of arguing, I tried flattery. I told Gramma that I had really enjoyed her stories, but I didn't have as good a memory as she did, and I was having trouble keeping all the details straight. When I stop to think about it, I guess I was telling the truth.

Anyway, it worked. Gramma blamed my poor memory on too much television, but agreed to go through the trunk with me again. We started that very evening and continued every day for the next two weeks. And I never got the stories mixed up again.

I followed my father's suggestion and took my tape recorder with me.

17

.... "Did you get Mr. Brockhurst a present?" Joel asked as he scuffed a stone
along the sidewalk.

I pretended to be disgusted. "You are a very shal-
low person, Joel Werner," I said. "You are obsessed
with presents."

Maybe he was; maybe he wasn't. To be truthful, I
didn't really care. I was just trying to change the subject.

It was the last day of school. That meant no classes.
The day was really just a time to clean out desks and
lockers, turn in textbooks, collect report cards, get
class pictures signed — and give the teacher a thank-
you gift. At least, that's how it had been in other grades.

But with Mr. Brockhurst, you couldn't be sure.
He didn't always do things the same way as other
teachers. He was unpredictable. Maybe that's part
of the reason I didn't like him much.

Nevertheless, I'd survived the year, which was a miracle as far as I was concerned. And surprisingly, it hadn't been completely unbearable. Mr. Brockhurst was no Mrs. Pauls, but once I got used to him he wasn't *too* bad. He'd read my journal, and I was never going to forgive him for that. On the other hand, he was also the one who'd told my parents about the JGS Detective Agency. So everything sort of balanced out.

The point is, I didn't hate him any more. However, I wasn't willing to admit that out loud, and that's why I didn't want to answer Joel's question.

"I got him one of those pens you wear around your neck," Joel volunteered, giving the stone a good kick. "You know — because Mr. Brockhurst can never remember where he put his."

I nodded.

"So?" Joel pressed. "Did *you* get him anything?"

I bent down to tie my runner, letting my hair fall forward so he couldn't see my face. I suspected my feelings were written all over it.

"My *mother* got him something," I said.

"What?"

I kept my eyes on my shoe and attempted a casual shrug. "I don't know. I didn't ask."

Joel hooted, and I looked up quickly, ready for a fight.

"What's so funny?"

"Oh, nothing," he said through a know-it-all grin.

Then he turned his back to me and chased after the stone again.

That last day, Mr. Brockhurst didn't do anything out of the ordinary — well, one thing, but it was good, so no one minded. We'd finished cleaning up the classroom, and he was about to hand out report cards, when there was a knock on the door, and a delivery person tottered in behind a huge stack of pizzas and about thirty cans of pop! We all stared at the pizzas and then at Mr. Brockhurst.

"For us?" one of the boys said.

Mr. Brockhurst smiled and nodded. "For being a great class and making my job easy and fun," he said. "Thanks."

As we stuffed our faces, Mr. Brockhurst opened his gifts. He didn't make a big fuss like lots of the teachers do, acting as if each present was the exact thing they'd been waiting for their whole lives. But he did seem to like everything. I'd told Joel I didn't know what my mother had bought, but, of course, I did. It was a coffee mug with the words *Teachers have class* written around the outside of it.

"Thanks very much, Annie," Mr. Brockhurst said, holding it up so everyone could see. "Now I won't have to use the chipped guest cups in the staff room."

I tried to look like the gift was no big deal, but there was a little part of me that was glad he liked it. I guess I was feeling generous. I even let him sign my class picture.

.... "Just one more meeting, and then there won't be another one until September!" I complained to my father when he picked me up from the JGS Detective Agency the following Saturday. Joel had left for summer camp right after school let out, so I was on my own. "What am I going to do for *six whole weeks*?" I whined. "Why do they have to cancel the meetings over the summer anyway?"

"Probably because most people go away on holidays," Dad replied.

"Are we going anywhere?" I said. We usually did something for a week or two, even if it was just camping on the Island, but I hadn't heard my parents mention anything at all.

Dad glanced sideways at me, and then turned his eyes back to the road.

"I don't know, Annie. Right now it doesn't look like it."

"Why?" I asked, even though I was pretty sure I already knew the answer.

Dad stole another look at me.

"It's tough with your grandmother," he said. Then he tried to make a joke. "Can you see her backpacking through the woods and crawling in and out of a sleeping bag? How about chopping wood for the fire?"

I understood what he was saying, but I didn't think it was fair that the rest of us had to miss out on a holiday because of Gramma.

The car got quiet for a minute, and then Dad

said, "Maybe what we'll do is take a few day trips instead. You know – do some things that we can all enjoy, like Butchart Gardens, horse-drawn buggy rides, and picnics in the park. I'm sure we can arrange for Gramma to stay at the Werners' a couple of times too, so you, Claire, your mother, and I can do some other things like kayaking and whale watching, maybe. What do you think of that idea?"

It wasn't exactly what I'd had in mind, but I knew my dad was trying his best, and I didn't want to hurt his feelings. "Sure," I said as cheerfully as I could manage. "That'll be good."

For the next few minutes I just listened to the radio and watched the trees and houses zip by.

Then I said, "Dad?"

"Mmm-hmm." His eyes were on the road, and his fingers were tapping on the steering wheel to the beat of the music.

"Do you think we – I mean, you and me – do you think we could get to one or two Shamrocks games too? It's going to be playoffs soon, and we haven't seen a single game yet."

Dad took his eyes off the road and grinned at me.

"As a matter of fact, I was thinking about that very thing myself just the other day. The project I've been working on at the office is finished now, so no more overtime – at least, not until the next big deadline comes along. So for sure, we're going to get to some games." He grinned again. "Consider it a date."

18

....One of the great things about my dad is that he keeps his word. He'd said we would go to see the Shamrocks play, and we did — that same week. He'd also said we'd have some outings as a family, and the very next Saturday we went to Butchart Gardens. We got there in late afternoon and toured the grounds, browsed the gift shop, had dinner at the restaurant, then went around the gardens again under the lights and watched the fireworks display.

It was fun. Even Gramma seemed to enjoy it. I'm not saying that she laughed or even smiled, but she didn't complain, and she even wore her teeth. Dad pushed her around in a wheelchair. I suggested Mom should ride in one too, so that she didn't get over-tired, but she laughed at my idea. I could tell she was starting to feel better. Since school had ended, Claire and I had been helping out with Gramma, and Mom was getting a lot more rest. It showed. She'd gained back some of the weight she'd lost, and the dark circles under her eyes had disappeared. She'd even started puttering around the yard again.

My mother is a gardening whiz. She can make anything grow. Plants other people think are dead, my mom can bring back to life. She's amazing. The neighbors are constantly asking her how to get rid of bugs and slugs, what type of tomatoes to plant, when to prune fruit trees, and how to keep geraniums over the winter. And my mother tells them. I don't think there's anything about gardening she doesn't know.

What I didn't realize was that my grandmother was the same. I guess that's because at home, she barely went out in the yard. But as we walked around Butchart Gardens, she and my mother gabbed non-stop about all the flowers, shrubs, and trees. I was surprised — and impressed. They even knew the Latin names for all the plants — without reading the little signs!

It really was a nice day. Claire and I didn't even argue. Dad was a bit quiet, but I thought that was because Mom and Gramma were doing all the talking. It wasn't until the next day that I discovered the real reason.

"Claire, Annie," he said after we'd finished up Sunday's lunch dishes, "let's go for a ride and give your mother and grandmother a chance to rest."

Sunday drives are pretty common in my family,

so I didn't find anything unusual about my father's suggestion — until my parents did their secret eye exchange thing, that is. Claire saw it too. She looked at me, and I looked at her. Something was up.

Dad didn't keep us in suspense long. We weren't even at the end of our street when he said, "You remember I told you that I'd put Gramma's name on waiting lists at a few nursing homes?"

He instantly had our attention.

"Well, I got a phone call from one of them yesterday morning," he went on. "There's an opening."

Suddenly the car was vibrating with Claire's anger. "You lied!" She hammered the headrest with her fist. "You said it would be two years!"

I could see my father's startled eyes in the rearview mirror.

"No, Claire." He shook his head. "I said it *might* be two years. There's no way of predicting these things for sure."

Claire flung herself back against the seat and crossed her arms angrily over her chest. Her face was red. "Well, I don't care!" she yelled. "You're not putting Gramma in a home. I won't let you!"

"Claire, don't make this harder than it already is," my father tried to reason with her.

"Why not?" she retorted. "Someone has to be on Gramma's side. Someone has to stick up for her. Don't you know what those places are like? Haven't you seen the news programs and documentaries on television? Old people get abused in nursing homes. They get ignored or ... or ... or even *worse*. The people who are supposed to be looking after them hurt them! They steal from them too! Do you want that to happen to Gramma?"

I had no idea what Claire was talking about. Obviously I hadn't seen any of the television programs she was referring to.

"Now just calm down," my father said. "You're getting yourself all worked up."

I stole a quick glance at my sister. Her face was blotchy, and her eyes were shiny wet. For the first time that I could ever remember, I felt sorry for her. She wasn't putting on an act to get her own way. She was really upset. She didn't want Gramma to go. I still didn't understand why, but Claire seemed determined to protect Gramma, and I had to respect her for that.

"This isn't that kind of a place," my father said, glancing back and forth between the rear-view mirror and the road. "This is a reputable nursing home with professional staff. I checked its credentials very carefully. Your grandmother will receive excellent care."

Claire didn't say a word, but from the ferocious look on her face, I could tell she wasn't convinced.

"You don't have to take my word for it," Dad added. He steered the car over to the side of the road and shut off the engine. Then he nodded toward a building complex across the street.

Claire and I both looked. *Sea Ridge Lodge —
Residence for Seniors* the sign read.

Dad reached for the door handle. "Come on,"
he said. "I want you girls to see this place for your-
selves."

19

....Claire had made nursing homes sound like prisons. But Sea Ridge Lodge certainly didn't look like a prison. Shaded by oak trees and surrounded by sculptured lawns and gardens, it reminded me more of a ritzy estate in the Uplands than a home for the elderly.

The thing I liked best was that it had lots of windows. That meant Gramma would still be able to sit and look outside. I was surprised to realize I cared about that. My grandmother must have grown on me more than I'd thought. I still wanted her out of my bedroom, but I didn't see why she shouldn't live somewhere nice. And from the outside, Sea Ridge Lodge seemed perfect.

We pushed open the heavy glass door and let ourselves into the building. It was like walking into a freezer.

"Nice air conditioning," Claire grumbled, rubbing her arms. "You'd have to be a polar bear to survive in here."

"It's not that bad," Dad said. "It only seems cold because we've been out in the sun. In a couple of minutes you won't even notice it any more."

We were standing in the doorway of what looked like a waiting room, and Dad gestured toward a couch. "You girls have a seat while I find someone to show us around." Then he headed across the hall to a glassed-in office.

But Claire didn't sit down. She stayed right where she was, blocking the doorway like a human speed bump, scowling in Dad's direction and hugging herself against the cold. She was obviously in one of her moods. She might as well have been carrying a sign that said, *Speak to me – and die!*

I took a chair on the far side of the room and buried my face in a magazine.

When Dad returned a few minutes later, there was a lady with him. She was pretty in an untouchable sort of way. Her hair, makeup, clothes – even her smile – were perfect.

"Ms. Morrison, I'd like you to meet my daughters, Claire and Annie. Girls, this is Ms. Morrison, the director of Sea Ridge. She's going to give us a tour and explain the services the lodge provides."

Then Dad smiled, so I smiled too, but Claire didn't take the hint. Instead, she stared daggers at the woman.

If Ms. Morrison noticed, she didn't let on.

"How nice to meet you both," she gushed, extending her hand. I shook it. It was cold and bony. Claire turned away before Ms. Morrison got to her.

"Why don't we begin with the solarium," the director suggested, ignoring Claire's rudeness and leading the way down the hall. "Our residents love it there, especially on days like today."

I could see why. The solarium was all glass and tropical plants — and it was toasty warm, untouched by the icy fingers of air conditioning. Sunshine seeped through tinted windows and sprawled lazily across the chairs, tables, and white linoleum floor.

And over the residents too. As Ms. Morrison had predicted, the solarium was filled with people — old people. I'd never seen so many white-haired, wrinkled human beings in one place before.

They were like a collection of wizened apple dolls, propped up in wheelchairs or huddled around tables with their walkers parked beside them. Many of them sat alone, unmoving — unbreathing, almost — staring with blank eyes at whatever they happened to be facing. Even the people arranged in groups seemed disconnected. They were all so still and quiet.

I couldn't help thinking of Gramma. How often had I seen *her* sitting like that?

Ms. Morrison squeezed the hand of a silver-haired lady sitting beside a potted palm. "Hello, Mrs. Wilson. How are you doing today?"

The woman didn't answer, but she smiled.

Then Ms. Morrison was on the move again, walking briskly through the room, talking to my father and the residents as she went. Ignoring a dirty look from my sister, I hurried to catch up.

"They can come to the solarium anytime during the day from eight in the morning until nine at night," Ms. Morrison was saying. "They can play cards or board games, visit with family, read, chat with the other residents, or simply relax quietly and take in the view." She nodded toward a young woman helping a man up from one of the tables. "There is always a staff member on duty here."

We'd come full circle and were heading back into the hall. Over my shoulder I took one last look at the solarium. Mrs. Wilson was still sitting by the potted palm. And she was still smiling.

Our next stop was the dining room. Nothing special as far as I could tell — just a lot of tables and chairs. The kitchen, however, was a different matter. A bunch of people wearing white uniforms and hair nets were flying around the stainless steel room, chopping and whipping and straining huge quantities of food. Ms. Morrison was explaining about mealtimes and special diets, but it was kind of boring, so I listened to the music playing on a radio instead.

Sea Ridge Lodge was a big place, and we saw every inch of it, from the hypoallergenic detergent in the laundry room to the computer-operated furnace in the basement. Ms. Morrison was a very thorough guide.

As we were leaving the exercise area, my father said, "Ms. Morrison, I wouldn't want to intrude on anyone's privacy, but do you think it would be possible to view one of the residents' rooms? I think my daughters would like to see the type of accommodation their grandmother will have."

Ms. Morrison looked surprised and then apologetic. "I'm so sorry," she said. "Of course, they would. I wasn't thinking. I just assumed that because *you* had seen the residents' rooms before ..." She stopped and smiled her Miss America smile. "Never mind. It's my mistake. I'll show you right now." Then she did a quick about-face and headed down the hall in the opposite direction. She crooked her finger at us. "Come along. Your grandmother's room is this way." She made a sudden left turn, pointing to a sign overhead. "This is the men's wing. The women's rooms are on the other side of the community living area. We're taking a shortcut."

The corridor was very wide, with thick, flat, metal handrails running the length of both walls. An old man sat in a wheelchair outside one of the rooms. Ms. Morrison slowed as she approached him and called out in her cheery voice, "Good afternoon, Martin. What are you doing out here all by yourself? Waiting for the ladies to come by?"

Martin's eyes crinkled at the joke, and he gurgled

something, but it was impossible to tell what he'd said. A trickle of drool escaped from the corner of his mouth and started down his chin. When he made no move to stop it, Ms. Morrison pulled a tissue from her pocket and wiped it away. Then she patted the old man's shoulder and said, "I'll see you at dinnertime. Don't you be late now, it's your favorite tonight." And she was off again, while Martin mumbled something indecipherable after her.

I was fascinated and horrified at the same time. Martin had to be at least ninety years old, yet Ms. Morrison had spoken to him as if he were a child. And the thing was, he hadn't minded.

"Did you see that?" Claire muttered. "She treated that poor man like he was an idiot! He's old, not insane." She contorted her face into a sneer. "That's disgusting!"

But Dad had already caught up to Ms. Morrison, so I was the only one near enough to hear Claire.

She looked back at Martin, and her expression softened. Then she hissed into my ear, "Is this what you want for Gramma?"

I was stunned. Claire made it sound as if putting Gramma in a nursing home was my idea. I wanted to protest, but I couldn't find the words. By the time I finally did, Claire had stalked off, and I was left mumbling to myself.

Why was I the bad guy? I hadn't told a single person — not even Joel — about my secret wish for my grandmother to move out. But I felt guilty just the same.

We came to a stop in front of room 143W. Ms. Morrison unlocked the door and pushed it open.

As I peered inside, I almost fell over from shock. It was so small!

"Well, what do you think?" Ms. Morrison beamed at us.

I stared back at her dumbly. Did she really expect an answer?

The room contained a skinny bed, a night table, a chest of drawers, and a chair. Anything more would have been too much. In one corner there was a small clothes cupboard. Halfway along the wall a gray accordion door opened into a closet size bathroom containing a toilet and sink.

And that was it. This was what my grandmother would call home until ... until forever. Suddenly I felt sick.

"Of course, residents are more than welcome to bring in their own belongings," Ms. Morrison purred.

And put them where? I thought about all of Gramma's things. There wasn't even room for her heirloom trunk.

"Bedspreads, window dressings, ornaments – that sort of thing," Ms. Morrison explained. "The only exception is floor coverings."

I glanced down at the linoleum. It was white like the floor of the solarium.

"We ask that no carpeting, rugs, or mats of any kind be brought in. I admit, they add a homey touch, but it is our experience that they are unsafe and unhygienic." She offered us a sympathetic smile. "I'm sure you understand."

I didn't, but my father nodded, so I kept quiet. I poked my head into the tiny bathroom.

"Where is the bathtub?" I asked.

"Facilities are staggered along the hallway. Bathing is supervised — again, for the safety of the residents."

An image of my grandmother in her robe, lined up in the hallway outside one of the shower rooms, popped into my head.

Claire grumbled something. I glanced around the cramped room again. On the wall above the light switch was a no-smoking decal.

I turned to Ms. Morrison and pointed to the sign. "The lady who had this room before — was she a non-smoker?"

Ms. Morrison seemed surprised. "Oh, no. I mean, I have no idea. The no-smoking signs are posted in all the rooms. Sea Ridge Lodge is a smoke-free facility."

20

.... "Well?" Dad said when we'd returned to the car. "What do you think? Is Sea Ridge Lodge a good place?"

I braced myself, waiting for Claire to explode, but all she did was scowl at Dad for a few seconds and then look away.

It was my father who lost his temper.

"What's that supposed to mean?" he snapped. "I asked you a question. I'd appreciate an answer."

"Why?" Claire spat back. "You don't care what I think! You've already made up your mind, so why bother asking my opinion? Anyway, I've told you how I feel. Gramma belongs with us. Put her in *there*," she pointed angrily toward the lodge, "and she's just another mouth to feed, another bed to change. Sure, the place looks nice, but it's not a home, and the people who work there aren't family. If you put

Gramma in a nursing home, all she'll be is somebody's job, and all she'll be doing is waiting to die."

There was a sickening silence.

Eventually my father said, "I see." And then, quietly, "Annie, what about you?"

I was so surprised, my knees nearly gave out. What *about* me? I'd sort of come to think of myself as an invisible observer in all of this. Oh, I had thoughts, all right, but I hadn't realized anybody wanted to know what they were. And I wasn't sure I wanted to tell them.

"How do you feel about Gramma moving to a nursing home?"

I licked my lips. Where should I begin? Originally, all I'd wanted was for Gramma to go away. I hadn't cared where, just as long as she moved out of our house. But it wasn't that easy any more.

I tried to push my own concerns to the back of my thoughts and consider Sea Ridge Lodge with my grandmother's needs in mind. To begin with, the building was new and clean, and it had just about every convenience that existed. There were other old people for Gramma to make friends with, and there were lots of activities for her to do. Most important of all, the people who worked there were trained nurses, they were friendly, and they truly seemed to care about the residents.

Then I thought about our house. It really wasn't "senior citizen friendly" at all. And there were scatter mats everywhere! Not only that, there was nothing for Gramma to do and no one her age to talk to.

It was no contest. Sea Ridge Lodge could take way better care of Gramma than we could.

But would she be happy there? That was the part I wasn't sure about.

"Did you like Sea Ridge Lodge, Annie?" my father broke into my thoughts.

I looked at him. My face couldn't decide whether to smile or frown. "Yes," I answered cautiously. Claire clucked her tongue in disgust. "And no," I added.

Dad's eyebrows twisted together. "What do you mean?"

I had a feeling that no matter what I said, it was going to come out wrong.

"Well," I heaved a huge sigh, "it *seems* like a good place. It probably has everything Gramma needs ..." I paused again. "And I bet the people there would take really good care of her ..."

"But?" my father said. "I hear a *but*."

I fidgeted and looked down at my feet. "But I don't think Gramma would like it there."

I couldn't believe I was saying that. For one thing, it meant I was siding with my sister. But more importantly, if my father really cared what Claire and I thought, it could mean I would never get my room back.

My father's frown deepened. "Why do you think that?"

What could I say? The room was too small?

Gramma should have her own bathtub? She'd have to quit smoking? The people there were strangers? It was all those things, but it was more than that. It had only been an uncomfortable gnawing at the back of my mind until Claire had attached words to it. But now that she had, I couldn't unknow it again.

Putting Gramma in a nursing home would be like telling her she didn't matter any more. But knowing that and finding words to say it were two different things.

"Gramma will think we don't love her," I said lamely.

"But we *do* love her!" Dad's face collapsed. "We just can't take care of her properly. If we continue to try looking after her ourselves, there is going to be an accident."

There was another suffocating silence. Then my father took hold of Claire's hand and mine. His eyes were shiny with tears when he began speaking again.

"Old age is a sneaky thing. It creeps up on you while you're busy living. You don't even notice, until one day, there it is. It doesn't matter how rich you are, how powerful you are, how good a person you are — you get old. Maybe it wouldn't be so bad if you got gray hair and wrinkles and slowed down a bit, until you just slipped away. But that's not usually what happens.

"People wear out. And the longer they live, the more things go wrong. Bones get brittle, reflexes slow down, hearing and sight become impaired, thinking becomes muddled — and on and on it goes, until ..."

He paused and took a deep breath.

"But human beings are amazing creatures. We can fool ourselves into believing nothing has changed. Maybe that's the mind's way of compensating for the parts that don't work any more."

Dad paused and squeezed our hands.

"Gramma is eighty-one. She is an old woman. Her body and her mind have started letting her down. And it's only going to get worse. She needs care that you, your mother, and I just can't give her."

He looked up at the sky.

"Never in my life did I imagine I would be in this position. Committing my mother to a nursing home is the hardest thing I shall probably ever have to do. You can't begin to know how much it hurts me." My father's voice all but disappeared. "It is ripping my heart out."

A tear rolled down his cheek. He let go of our hands and brushed it away.

My own heart felt as if someone had walked on it. I ached for my dad as he must have been aching for Gramma.

Claire threw her arms around him and buried her face against his shoulder. "I'm sorry, Dad."

He hugged her and kissed the top of her head. Then he reached out with his other arm and pulled me close too.

We stood outside the car that way for the longest time, hugging one another and feeling awful.

21

.... Arrangements were made for Gramma to see the lodge on Wednesday. If she liked it, she could move in the following Sunday. But on Tuesday evening, all that changed.

That night is still a blur to me. One minute Gramma was complaining that supper had given her indigestion, and the next minute she was slumped in her chair, Dad was bent over her, and Mom was dialing 911. Then there were sirens and flashing lights, and paramedics in our dining room, wrapping Gramma in blankets, strapping her to a stretcher, and rushing her and Dad away in an ambulance.

Claire and I rode to the hospital with Mom, but after hours of waiting in the emergency area without any news, our parents sent us back home in a cab. It was the longest night of my life — Claire's too, I guess. We didn't even bother going to bed. We just sat on the couch in the living room, staring at the phone.

It wasn't until the next morning that we finally heard anything. The doctors said Gramma had had a heart attack, and she was very sick.

My aunt and uncle flew out from Winnipeg and camped at the hospital with my parents. As for Claire and I, we didn't see Gramma again until Friday.

She looked awful. Lying in that big hospital bed, with machines all around her and tubes coming out of her nose and arms, she seemed so small and fragile. I was afraid to touch her in case she broke.

We didn't stay long — maybe ten minutes — and although Claire and I did most of the talking, the visit seemed to wear Gramma out. Claire stood on one side of her bed and I stood on the other, and Gramma held our hands the whole time. She didn't even want to let go when we had to leave.

"Come back again," she said, and we promised we would.

The next time we visited her, she looked a bit better, and she asked me how the family tree was shaping up. Even though there were no JGS meetings over the summer, I was trying to hunt down clues on my own. I had a stack of art books from the library, which I hoped might tell me something about the porcelain miniature. I told my grandmother that if I found any leads, she'd be the first to know.

Inspired by my promise, I hauled out the art books

as soon as I got home. Dad said it would be okay if I used the miniature from Gramma's trunk to help me with my search, so I dug that out too. I really wanted to find another piece to the puzzle before I visited my grandmother again. She had told me so much about our family, I wanted to give her something back — something she cared about. I thought it might cheer her up and help her to get better.

If I could find out who had painted the miniature, that would be a big help. Unfortunately, all the artist had been able to squeeze in at the bottom of the tiny portrait were the initials CWP. I checked out the indexes. There were quite a few painters whose last names began with P, but the C and W didn't fit.

So much for that idea. Now I had no choice but to plow through the books one page at a time. I surveyed the stack in front of me and cringed. This could take hours!

But if I found something out, it would be worth it. There'd be another family story for Gramma to add to her heirloom trunk. In my mind, I imagined how she would react when I finally uncovered the mystery behind the picture and the letter. She'd probably frown and grumble and pretend she didn't care. I smiled to myself. Gramma could be as grumpy as she liked. Underneath, she'd be pleased. I was sure of it.

With renewed determination, I pulled the pile of

books toward me and began flipping through the glossy photographs. The clothing and hairstyle of the woman on the porcelain miniature seemed a lot like the ones worn by women in the 1700s.

Most of the books were organized in time periods, so it wasn't too hard to locate the eighteenth-century paintings. But considering that the miniature had been in my family since before there were cameras, it was unlikely I was going to find a photograph of it in an art book. So, really, I had no idea what I was looking for.

Maybe that's why I didn't find anything. Two hours later, I slapped shut the last art book and flopped back dejectedly in my chair. For all I knew, I had passed right by a clue and not even known it. I found myself wishing Gordon was here. He'd know what to look for.

Then I sat up straight again. Gordon *would* know. So why not ask him? There might not be any JGS meetings during the summer, but that didn't mean Gordon wouldn't help me.

Well, there was only one way to find out, I decided, and hauled out the telephone book.

.... When I got off the phone, I was excited again. Gordon had said he would be happy to help me track down William and Constance. Of course, he would need to see the miniature and the letter — he said there were probably all kinds of clues hiding in things like the style of the miniature's frame and the type of ink and paper used in the letter. From what I'd told him, though, he suspected William might have been a Loyalist, and perhaps that was why he and Constance had been separated. Gordon said there was a good chance we might get a lead from the list of Loyalists who had been granted land when they'd moved to Canada.

Gordon was going out of town for a few days, but he promised he'd call when he got back, and then we'd start digging. I could hardly wait.

22

....I visited my grandmother again the next day. She seemed a lot better. She still looked weak and tired, and she was still hooked up to machines, but she was sitting up in bed, and there was color in her cheeks.

I told her about Gordon's Loyalist theory and how he was going to help me in my search. To my surprise – and disappointment – Gramma didn't seem very impressed.

"You're still no further ahead," she told me bluntly.

"Sure I am," I protested. "I know that William might have been a Loyalist who moved to Canada, and if Gordon and I can track down the portrait artist and where the frame was made, we might be able to find out who the lady in the miniature is. I bet you anything it's the Constance in William's letter."

"But you don't know."

"Well ... not for sure," I admitted.

"There you are." The tone of Gramma's voice said there was no point in going on with the discussion.

But I wasn't ready to give it up. I was positive Gordon and I were going to uncover something important, and I was determined to make my grandmother see that.

"You wait, Gramma," I insisted. "I *am* going to find out. You'll see. And I bet it doesn't take long at all. Gordon is really good at this stuff, and he says there are lots of places we can go for clues. Just think how neat it'll be when we finally have the answers."

But my grandmother sniffed and changed the subject. "Hmmph," she said. "Look how pale you are. You're spending too much time indoors with books. You should be outside, playing in the sunshine."

"It's raining, Gramma," I pointed out, "and it has been almost all week."

"So? Will you shrink if you get wet?" She tried to glare at me, but she didn't have the strength.

I didn't push. "Sorry," I said. "You're right."

She closed her eyes and melted against the pillows. When she stayed that way for several minutes, I thought she must have dozed off, but then she began talking again.

"I love the rain," she murmured. Her eyes were still shut, but something like a smile was playing at the corners of her mouth. "Especially a spring rain. Don't you?"

She didn't pause long enough for me to answer.

"It soaks the soil black," she inhaled deeply, "and that glorious earthy smell makes the inside of your nose tingle. The next thing you know, fat orange-breasted robins are hopping through the rain-speckled grass, listening for juicy worms to come a little too close to the surface. And then you blink, and suddenly everything comes alive. You can practically see the crocuses and tulips and daffodils pushing up through the ground, and the buds opening on the trees." Then she laughed.

It would be an understatement to say I was surprised. Never before — *not even once!* — in the whole time my grandmother had lived with us, had I heard her laugh. It was a wonderful sound — almost like flute music. It made me feel warm all over.

"What are you grinning at?" she demanded, but there wasn't the usual clipped annoyance in her voice.

I sobered. How had she known I'd been smiling? Her eyes were still closed.

Then I got my answer. "Oh, Tom," she said, "stop being an old stick-in-the-mud. Come walk with me in the rain. It's lovely." She laughed again. "So what if we get wet? I doubt very much that we'll shrink."

That's when I realized Gramma wasn't speaking to me. She was caught up in a memory of Grandpa Tom.

I sat quietly, waiting for her to say something else, but she didn't. And after a few minutes her breathing changed, and I could tell she had drifted off to sleep, so I tiptoed out of the room.

.... I couldn't seem to get that visit out of my mind. I think it was because it made me wonder if I had been wrong about my grandmother.

The sour, critical old lady with a knack for saying hurtful things — *that* Gramma I knew. But who was this person who laughed like an angel and liked walking in the rain? Certainly not *my* grandmother! Fiona Granville couldn't laugh any more than she could fly.

Or could she? Was it possible that after living with her for nearly six months, I still didn't know who she was?

My father didn't see her the way I did. I knew that. I'd never been able to understand how he could have such a soft spot for her, but then I'd never heard Gramma laugh before — or speak to anyone without snapping. But when she'd thought she was talking to Grandpa Tom, she'd sounded just like my mom when she's teasing my dad.

The thought gave me a jolt. *What was the matter with me?* I had just compared Gramma to my mother!

Then I started to think. Hadn't my father said they were alike too — the day he'd been talking to Mom in the garage? Of course, I hadn't believed it.

The idea still bothered me, but not for quite the

same reason. Back then, all I knew was that my grandmother was a crotchety old woman, and I never ever wanted my mother to end up like that. So I had refused to believe it could happen. It was more comfortable to think Gramma had always been grumpy and stubborn.

But now I wasn't so sure.

I had heard my grandmother laugh, and when she'd thought she was talking to Grandpa, there'd been mischief in her voice. She liked watching robins, she believed she could see flowers grow, and she enjoyed walking in the rain! I hadn't known any of those things! In fact, I was beginning to realize that I didn't know my grandmother at all — not my *real* grandmother.

But my parents did — even Claire seemed to. I felt cheated. I'd only had the tiniest peek at the person my grandmother must have been, but it was enough to convince me I had missed out on something wonderful. It also made me determined to get to know her better — if she'd let me. Age had made Gramma different, but the true Fiona Granville must still be in there somewhere, and I was going to find her.

In my mind, I heard Gramma laugh again, and I wondered if *she* realized how much she'd changed.

I hoped not.

23

.... Samson tore across the park, leaped into the air and caught the Frisbee in his mouth. Then he trotted proudly back and dropped it at Joel's feet.

"Doesn't he ever get tired of chasing that thing? He's been doing it for nearly half an hour."

Joel hurled the Frisbee again, and Samson charged after it.

"He loves to run. He could do this all day."

I watched as Samson snatched the spinning disk out of the air.

"He's really good," I said. "I haven't seen him miss once."

"And you don't want to." Joel made a face. "He gets into a really bad mood when he drops it."

"Get out!" I gave Joel a shove. "Animals don't get into moods."

"Sure they do. Look at Sandy and Sandy. They were super-depressed when you first brought them over to my house."

"Really?" I didn't want my gerbils to be depressed, but it was sort of comforting to think they'd missed me.

"For sure." Joel flicked the Frisbee into the sky again. "Heck, one of them got such a bad migraine, I had to close the blinds and put a cold cloth over its eyes."

I should have seen that coming. Joel hadn't made a joke in almost fifteen minutes. He was way overdue. I shook my head. "You need help."

"Nah," he waved away my remark. "I wouldn't know what to do with an assistant." Then he grinned. Nobody likes Joel's jokes better than he does.

I rolled my eyes. "Has anyone ever told you you're warped?"

He pretended I'd hurt his feelings. "Is that the thanks I get for turning my bedroom into a daycare center for your gerbils?" He picked the Frisbee up from the grass where Samson had dropped it. "This is the last time, fella," he told the dog. "Maybe *you* don't get tired, but my arm's gonna fall off."

When Samson was once more galloping across the field, Joel turned back to me. "I guess you won't be needing my services much longer, though, will you? If your granny's going to be moving into a nursing home, you'll be able to take Sandy and Sandy back to your place."

I nodded. I hadn't been thinking about that lately.

"How's your granny doing, anyway?" Joel asked.

We started toward the park exit.

"Lots better. She's probably going to be released from the hospital in a couple of days."

"Will she be coming back to your house?"

Trust Joel to get right to the point. He wasn't a person to tiptoe around touchy subjects.

I shook my head. "I don't think so. My parents haven't come right out and said anything for sure, but Dad told us there was no point in prolonging the inevitable. He says the change is going to be hard enough as it is. It wouldn't be fair to bring Gramma home and then move her again."

We walked in silence for a few minutes before Joel said, "Are you going to miss her?"

A few months ago — even a few weeks ago — my answer would have been a very loud and definite no. But now the word stuck in my throat. Instead, I said, "We're going to visit her all the time, and Dad said Gramma can come with us to dinner or a movie whenever she wants."

Joel nodded. We kept walking.

After a while I said, "I'm going to spend more time with my grandmother. I want to get to know her better."

Out of the corner of my eye I could see Joel studying me curiously.

"Oh, I get it," he said finally. "You wanna get

more information for your family tree."

I whirled on him. "No! That's not it at all!"

Joel frowned and took a step back. "What's with you? It's obvious you're not crazy about your grandmother. You never have been. If it weren't for JGS, the two of you probably *still* wouldn't be talking. So what other reason — besides your family tree — could you have for spending time with her?"

I felt my cheeks turning to fire. I didn't want to talk about this.

But Joel didn't seem to notice. He came at me again like a reporter for *The National Enquirer.* "Why the big change of heart?"

I couldn't bring myself to look at him. I didn't understand what I was feeling myself. How was I supposed to explain it to him?

I shrugged, hoping he'd let it go. But he didn't, of course.

"Are you feeling guilty — or what?"

I scowled at him. "Why should I feel guilty?"

Joel shrugged. "I don't know. I guess because your granny nearly died. People always feel guilty about stuff like that."

Joel was closer to the truth than I was willing to admit, and more than ever, I wanted out of the conversation. Thank goodness we'd reached the bottom of my driveway.

"I gotta go," I said, bolting across the lawn. I didn't want him to think I was mad, though, so when

I got to the front steps, I waved and yelled, "Call me after supper." Then I quickly let myself into the house.

It was strangely quiet.

"Mom?" I poked my head into the living room. It felt odd not to see Gramma sitting on the couch. I wandered through the dining room to the kitchen. "Mom?" I called again, but there was still no answer. I peered out the window. She wasn't in the yard either.

I went back to the living room and looked out at the driveway. Her car was gone. Strange I hadn't noticed that when I came in. I guess I'd been concentrating on getting away from Joel and his questions.

I flopped down onto the couch and tried to think where my mother could have gone. Then I remembered her saying something that morning about picking up my father's suits at the cleaners.

I grabbed the remote from the coffee table and aimed it at the television. Instantly the screen came to life, and voices blasted the quiet afternoon to bits, ricocheting off the walls and attacking my eardrums with sledgehammers. Using one hand to cover my ears, I fumbled for the volume button with the other.

As the voices took on a human level again, I sagged against the cushions of the couch and shut my eyes.

When I opened them, I found myself looking straight into the angry face of my sister. I shrank away from her, though there really wasn't anywhere to go.

"It wasn't my fault," I said before she could attack. "The volume was already up when I turned the television on."

Claire shook her head.

"It was! Honest," I insisted.

She pulled the remote out of my hand and clicked off the set. Then, in a voice that sounded as if she'd swallowed barnacles, she said, "I need to talk to you." She dropped down beside me on the couch, cleared her throat and swiped at her nose with a tissue.

"Are you getting a cold?"

She shook her head.

"Because if you are, stay away from —"

"Annie, shut up and listen!"

That was when I knew something was wrong — not because Claire had told me to shut up. She'd said worse things than that to me before. It was the way she said it that caught my attention. I looked at her more closely. Her eyes were red and puffy, and her eyelashes were stuck together in wet clumps. She wasn't angry at all. And she didn't have a cold either. She'd been crying.

She wiped her nose again and took a ragged breath.

"Mom had to go to the hospital."

I instantly panicked. "Why? What's the matter with her?"

Claire shook her head, and tears started spilling from her eyes. "Nothing. Dad is meeting her there.

She went to the hospital because somebody called about Gramma."

My next thought was that my grandmother must be coming home, and my parents had gone to pick her up, but why would my sister be crying about that?

Claire blew her nose once more and wiped her tears away before continuing. It was hard for her to speak. She sounded like someone was choking her, and the words came out in gasps. "Gra ... Gra ... Gramma ... ha ... ad ... another ... heart attack."

What was she talking about? Gramma was getting better. The hospital was going to release her. She couldn't have had another heart attack. There had to be some sort of mistake.

I tried to calm my sister. "Don't cry, Claire. The hospital must have gotten Gramma mixed up with somebody else."

Claire shook her head and sobbed. I'd never seen her so upset. She was crying so hard now, she couldn't stop.

"No, Annie. It's ... it's true."

Suddenly I began to worry. I didn't want to believe what Claire was telling me, but she wouldn't fall to pieces for no reason at all.

"Don't worry," I said gruffly. One of us had to be strong. "If Gramma's had another heart attack, she'll get over it just like she did the other one."

At that, Claire's face totally caved in. "Oh, Annie.

No!" she wailed. "She won't. She can't." She sobbed
again. "Don't you see?"

I had a sick feeling that I was beginning to.

Claire mopped away the latest flood of tears rolling down her cheeks, then grabbed my arm.

"Gramma's gone, Annie. She died."

24

.... For the next few days, the world went numb. Everything seemed to be happening in slow motion, and I felt like I was sitting on the ceiling, watching. Gramma had died, and the rest of us had turned into robots. Our bodies kept doing the things they'd always done — eating, showering, taking out the garbage — but it didn't feel like we were inside them.

And then there was the funeral. It wasn't what I'd expected at all.

For one thing, the weather was wrong. The sun was shining and the sky was blue. It should have been raining.

For another thing, there was too much color. People are supposed to wear black to funerals — black suits, black dresses, black hats, black veils. Maybe even black underwear. But judging from my grandmother's funeral, not many people knew the rule.

In fact, not many people came. There was almost no one there — only Mom, Dad, Claire and me, my aunt and uncle, a few of my parents' friends, and some of our neighbors. The chapel wasn't all that big, but we didn't even begin to fill it. I felt bad for my grandmother. She'd lived nearly eighty-two years, and hardly anyone had shown up to say good-bye.

The service didn't last long. An organist played some hymns and the minister read from the Bible. Then he talked about Gramma. That's the part of the funeral that bothered me most. Reverend Willis had never even met my grandmother, yet he stood by her casket at the front of the chapel, rambling on as if she'd been a member of his congregation forever. And the thing was, he said stuff that I hadn't known. I was finding out about my grandmother from a stranger!

Afterwards, people came back to our house. Mom put out sandwiches and sweets, as well as juice and pots of tea and coffee. At first everyone was quiet, smiling self-consciously and offering my parents whispered condolences. Then my father opened a bottle of Scotch he'd been saving for years, and Gramma's funeral turned into a party. All through our house, people were talking up a storm — and laughing!

"Do you remember the time Mom was painting one of the upstairs bedrooms, and we scared the heck out of her?" Uncle Mark laid a hand on my father's shoulder and chuckled.

Dad's face split into a grin. "How could I forget? If she'd caught us, she would have killed us."

Uncle Mark rubbed his chin, and his whiskers made a scratchy sound. "Seems to me, we wanted to go to the movies, but we needed her permission." He frowned. "It beats me how we could have surprised her, though. As I recall, we were never that quiet."

"Don't you remember?" my father said. "She'd given us strict instructions not to bug her. So we figured that if we stomped up the stairs, she'd get annoyed, and then we wouldn't be allowed to go."

Uncle Mark's expression cleared. "That's right. We must have stood in the doorway a good three or four minutes — just watching her. She was down on her haunches, painting the baseboards. And the paint tray was right behind her. Remember? Then you said —"

"*Me!*" my father objected. "You're the one who did the talking."

My uncle laughed. "True. You never were any good at asking for things. You always managed to get us turned down. Anyway, Mom was so wrapped up in her painting, she had no idea we were standing there, and when we opened our mouths, she jumped a mile!"

Dad and Uncle Mark both started to howl. The other people listening to the story snickered too.

Dad choked back his laughter long enough to

say, "Then she lost her balance and fell backwards into the tray of paint!"

At that, everyone in the entire room erupted in laughter — even my mother.

It *was* a funny story, but I didn't crack a smile. It was disrespectful to make fun of the dead, and I wasn't having any part of it.

I backed away from the buzz of voices and, when no one was looking, slipped away to the room I shared with Claire. I hadn't thought I'd be missed, but after a few minutes, my mother came looking for me.

She sat down on the bed. "It's been a tough day, sweetie. I know." She put her arm around me and gave my shoulder a squeeze. "But never mind. It's nearly over."

I pulled away and scowled at her. "Why did you laugh?" It wasn't like my parents — especially my mother — to be so insensitive.

Her eyebrows lifted and then knotted together. "I don't know what you mean, dear."

"Just now — in the living room. You and Dad and everybody else were laughing at Gramma! How could you? This is her funeral, but you're all acting like it's a party! Gramma died! What's there to celebrate?"

Mom took my hands in hers and smiled her sad smile, the one that always means there *is* an explanation. So, even though she didn't say anything right away, I knew she was going to. I sat and waited. Finally, she began.

"When someone we love dies, Annie, we are overwhelmed with sadness. We are crippled by it. It's all we can think about. We can't carry on with any of our normal activities. We're not interested in eating, working, talking, playing — nothing seems important any more. All we can do is hurt. That's called grieving. And that's what you and Claire and me — and especially your father — have been doing since Gramma passed away."

Mom took a huge breath before continuing.

"And that's okay. Grieving is necessary. It's how we work through our feelings — but it can't go on forever. That wouldn't be healthy. The sadness doesn't all of a sudden disappear, but it fades with time. It'll be a while before any of us can think of Gramma without hurting, but each day the pain will become a little less."

Mom paused again, and I thought about what she'd said. Was *I* grieving? I'd cried when Gramma died, but not the same way Claire had. Still, my heart felt like a lump of lead, and I seemed to be in a bad mood all the time. And I couldn't stop thinking about Gramma. If that was grieving, I guess I was doing it.

My mother licked her lips and carried on.

"A funeral is a sort of turning point. It tells us to let that healing process begin. It is also a time to honor the person who has died. That's what we're doing today — we're honoring Gramma. What better way to do that than to remember the good times? Hmm?"

I hadn't thought about funerals like that.

"Your father and uncle — and the rest of us — we weren't making fun of Gramma, Annie. We were reliving happy memories of her. We were sharing the love we felt for Gramma with each other. We were showing how thankful we are to have been a part of her life." Her eyes were glistening with tears. "So when you say it looked like we were celebrating — you were right. We were. We were celebrating Gramma's life."

..............................My mother must have been right about the funeral being a turning point, because the very next day, things started getting back to normal. It wasn't like we suddenly forgot about Gramma and everything was fine again, but Dad did go back to work, Claire and I had an argument, and when the organizers of a telethon asked Mom to help, she said she would.

The day after that, Joel brought my gerbils back. I was out at the time. In fact, everyone was out — everyone except Claire. When I saw Joel in the park a little while later, he told me he'd dropped them off. Of course, he was all proud of himself. I, on the other hand, was having a fit. Knowing how my sister felt about my gerbils, I was sure I was never going to see them again.

I ran all the way home without stopping and burst into the house so ferociously that the front door crashed into the wall and then me. Holding my head and gasping for air, I staggered to the living room. Claire was watching television.

"What have you done with my gerbils?" I panted.

She never even looked up.

"Well?" I demanded. I wasn't going to let her ignore me.

She let out a huge sigh. "If you must know, I breaded them. They're in the toaster oven. Should be done in about two minutes."

"What?!" I grabbed onto the doorway for support.

Claire leaned against the cushions of the couch and shook her head. "You are so gullible." Then she rolled her eyes. "Try the bedroom."

I flew down the hall and skidded into the room. There was no telling where Claire had put my gerbils. Urgently, I scanned the debris. At last my eyes came to rest on my dresser. There was the cage, right on top, and inside were Sandy and Sandy, busily cracking sunflower seeds and burrowing through the wood shavings.

And there wasn't a sign of a breadcrumb anywhere.

25

.... For so many months, it had seemed that my entire life and happiness had depended on getting my bedroom back, and I would have done almost anything to make that happen. But after my grandmother died, I could barely stand to walk past my old bedroom, let alone move into it again.

I knew it wouldn't be the same. Even if it looked exactly like it had before, it wouldn't be the same. Because I wasn't the same. I wanted to be, but I knew I wasn't. Too many things had happened. I'd lost Mrs. Pauls and lived through Mr. Brockhurst. History Repeats Itself had folded. My mother had become ill. My grandmother had died. I hadn't wanted any of those things to happen, but they had. And moving back into my bedroom couldn't undo them.

So I looked straight ahead when I walked past the closed door, and I tried not to think about it.

The funny thing was, no one else brought the subject up either — not even Claire. I had a feeling it had something to do with what Mom had said about grieving. Healing took time, and none of us was ready to move Gramma out of that room. So we ignored it.

It had been a roller-coaster summer — especially the last two weeks after Gramma died — but it was finally coming to an end. School would be starting in less than a week, and the Junior Genealogical Society meetings would get underway the Saturday after that — only I had decided I wasn't going back.

Digging into the past would only make me think of my grandmother, and that hurt too much. My parents and sister might have had happy memories of Gramma, but all I had were regrets.

That was another thing I tried not to think about. But it's tough not thinking about things. At least, I'm not very good at it.

The weekend before school started, Mom took Claire and me to Vancouver. She said we could all use a change of scenery, and since we needed new clothes and books for school, we might as well get them there. I wasn't really all that excited about going, but it turned out okay, because — for some reason — my worries didn't come with me.

We stayed at the Hotel Vancouver and shopped for two solid days. Mom must have taken us to every store in the city! We even looked at things we had no intention of buying — like fur coats and wedding gowns. Mom tried on rings at a swanky jewelry store and asked them to hold a diamond-studded band for the afternoon. If Dad had been there, he would have had a fit! Of course, my mother wasn't planning to buy the ring, but it was fun to pretend. On a side street, we discovered a hat shop and spent an entire hour trying on everything from safari helmets to turbans. Claire was crazy! With every hat, she became a different person. She had me laughing so hard my stomach ached.

We ate in restaurants and ordered from hotel room service. In the evenings we put our aching feet up in front of the television and pigged out on junk food. Claire liked not having to make the bed. I liked everything.

On Sunday we came home.

Poor Dad — for nearly an hour we bombarded him with stories of our great Vancouver adventure. We'd brought him back a couple of presents though, so I think he felt obligated to listen. But he laughed and asked questions and complimented us on our purchases, so maybe he didn't mind too much.

Finally, Mom said it was time to put everything away.

"What time is it?" Claire said. "I have to call Janice and Bonnie and let them know I'm back."

Dad glanced at his wrist, but the only thing there was a suntan mark.

"I guess I left my watch in Gramma's bedroom," he said. "The Diabetes Association phoned, looking for donations, so I was cleaning out the closet in there. But I kept catching my watch on things and took it off. Annie, would you get it for me, please? I think it's on top of the steamer trunk."

I wished he'd asked Claire to do it, but I didn't want to make a fuss, so I pushed myself up off the living room floor and headed down the hall. If I concentrated on the watch, I could be in and out of Gramma's room in a couple of seconds.

But that didn't happen. The instant I opened the door, I forgot all about my father's watch.

All I could do was stare.

It wasn't my grandmother's room any more. But it wasn't mine either. It was like I'd walked into a whole different world.

I stepped into the room, and my feet sank into a plush peach-colored rug. The walls were peach too, except where they joined the ceiling. That was a wide, scalloped border of floral wallpaper. The puffy valence over the window had a floral pattern too. So did the comforter on the bed. It was the most beautiful bed I'd ever seen, framed with white wicker on three sides so that it was actually more like a sofa than a bed. The rest of the furniture was wicker too, even the glass-topped desk.

"What do you think?"

I turned around. Mom and Dad and Claire were

standing in the doorway.

"*Wow*," I breathed. "It's gorgeous. Is it ... I mean ... is it for *me*?"

Dad pointed to the dresser. "Well, Sandy and Sandy certainly seem to think so."

I hadn't even noticed my gerbils there. But Dad was right. They were rustling around inside their cage, as happy as they'd ever been.

Claire put a hand on my shoulder. "It's nice, isn't it?" she said. "The walls look a little naked, though. I bought a couple of magazines in Vancouver, if you want some help getting started."

"It's good of you to offer, Claire," Dad cut in quickly. "But maybe *you'd* better keep them. I think one room decorated that way is enough."

Claire shrugged. "Fine with me. Anyway, I'm outta here. I have phone calls to make."

When she'd left, I turned to my parents.

"Thank you. Thank you so much," I said. "It's the most beautiful bedroom I've ever seen. It's like a picture in a decorating book." I hugged my mother, then my father. And suddenly I was crying.

Dad cleared his throat. "Are you okay about this, Annie? I mean, about moving back in here? Because if you're not, you don't have to, you know. We'll under-stand. It's just that the house is so small, and —"

"It's okay, Dad." I knew what my father was try-ing to say, but he didn't need to worry. I looked around the room again. There were no ghosts — not of my grandmother, and not of me. I walked around and touched everything, and then I sat down on the bed.

That's when I noticed Gramma's steamer trunk. It was sitting on the rug in front of the bed like a coffee table — as plain as day — yet I hadn't noticed it until that moment.

Had my father forgotten to take it away? I looked at him curiously.

He smiled. "Gramma wanted you to have it," he said. "She felt it would mean more to you than anyone else. She thought it might help you with the family tree."

I stared at the trunk. I didn't want it. I didn't care about my family tree any more. I had wanted to find answers while my grandmother was alive. I'd wanted to do it for her. Now that she was gone, I didn't care. All the trunk could do was remind me that I was never going to see Gramma again — and, even worse, that I was never going to know her.

I guess I had been hiding from my feelings for so long that they sneaked up on me, and suddenly I couldn't hold them back another second.

"I didn't want Gramma to live here," I blurted. The confession was out before I could stop it. I'm not sure how the words escaped, but suddenly I heard myself talking, and I was saying things I hadn't thought I would ever tell anyone. "She ruined everything. From the very first day she moved in, things started going wrong — my room, my gerbils, my teacher, Mom getting sick, History Repeats Itself — everything! So I blamed Gramma. I thought it was her fault, and I was sure that if she would just go away, things would be okay again."

I kept my eyes on my hands. I couldn't look at my parents. I was too ashamed.

"But I didn't want her to *die!*" I heard my voice crack and then misery was choking me, and I couldn't get out another word. The next thing I knew, my parents were beside me.

"Of course you didn't, Annie. Of course you didn't," my mother soothed me, stroking my hair.

"We know that, sweetheart," Dad said, squeezing my hand. "What you felt was perfectly natural."

"But I was so awful!" I blubbered. "I should have been nicer. I should have spent more time with Gramma. I didn't like her. She was my grandmother, but I didn't like her! I thought she was mean. I-I-I didn't know. I mean, I didn't know who she was, not really. And I didn't *try* to get to know her — not until the end. And then it was too late." I was crying hard now.

Dad hugged me.

"Don't be so tough on yourself," he said. "Your grandmother didn't make it easy to get close to her. When she got old, she got prickly. Considering you didn't know her at all before she came to live with us, you did just fine. She may have been grumpy, but don't be fooled. She loved you very much. That's one of the reasons she wanted you to have the trunk."

My mother passed me a tissue. I dabbed at my tears and gave my nose a good blow.

"You're just trying to make me feel better," I said.

"Of course I am." Dad gave me another squeeze. "But that doesn't mean I'm not telling the truth. If anyone knows how important Gramma's memories were to her, it should be you. You spent hours and hours listening to her stories."

I sniffed and nodded. "I thought if I could find out about the porcelain miniature and that old letter, it would make her happy."

"I'm sure it would have," Dad agreed.

"But I didn't get a chance." I started to cry again.

Dad held me at arm's length.

"You can still do it."

"It's too late now!" I wailed. "Gramma's gone. Even if I *could* find out about William and Constance, I can't tell her. So what's the point?"

"The point is, she would want you to. She cared about family and tradition. Don't you know how unhappy she would have been if she'd thought all that history was going to die when she did? When you came into Gramma's life, it was like an answer to a prayer. That's why she shared her stories with you. That's why she left you her trunk — to keep the past from being lost."

I stopped crying.

Was that true? Was Gramma counting on me?

Was she depending on me to keep the family history alive? And if she were, would I be able to do what she wanted? Suddenly it seemed like a huge responsibility. I wiped away my tears and looked up earnestly at my dad.

"Really?"

He nodded. "Really."

My grandmother had kept the family's treasures and secrets, hopes and memories, alive all these years, and now it was my turn to do the same. I took a deep breath and looked up at my father again. "Well," I said, "I guess I can try."

He smiled. "Your grandmother couldn't ask for more than that."

.... When my parents had gone, I sat on my new bed in my new room, staring at my grandmother's steamer trunk and thinking.

I *would* find out about William and Constance. And I would find out about my grandmother too — about the lady who'd been a nurse and a mother and who liked to laugh and walk in the rain. Her memory was alive in my parents, and I could learn about her through them. And what I learned, I would cherish — along with all the other memories she had entrusted to me.

I slid down onto the peach rug and opened the lid of the trunk. It looked just as it had the last time

Gramma had gone through it with me, except there was something else there now too — my tape recorder. I lifted it out and placed it on the rug beside me. Then I reached back into the trunk and picked up a tarnished silver napkin ring. It was cool and smooth in my hand.

Without thinking, I pushed the play button of the tape recorder, and my grandmother's voice filled the room.

"This was my napkin ring," she said. "Everyone in the family had one, and they were all different. That's so they didn't get mixed up. When I was growing up, there was no such thing as paper napkins. They were all cloth, and we had to use them over and over. There were no automatic washers and dryers back then like there are now, you know. So after every meal, we used to roll our napkins back up and put them inside our napkin rings until the next time.

"Anyway, mine was silver. My brother, George — his was carved ivory, and my sister, Helen, had a real beauty made of mahogany. My uncle had brought it back from Asia. Well, that mahogany napkin ring was my favorite. I don't know how many times I tried to convince my sister to trade with me, but she wouldn't. She could be a real sourpuss."

On the tape recorder, my voice replaced my grandmother's. "You *never* got her to trade with you?"

There was a pause, and in my mind I could see Gramma scowling at me, just as she had the evening she'd told me that story. "Isn't that what I just said?" she'd snapped. "Aren't you listening to me, child?"

At the time, I'd had to bite my tongue to keep from talking back. But now, I just smiled.

"Yes, Gramma," I replied softly to the tape recorder. "I'm listening."

And I was.

Destrubé Photography

MEET KRISTIN BUTCHER

Many writers have been teachers. I'm not quite sure why that is, but it is and I'm no exception. I taught for twenty years — everything from primary science and intermediate math to junior high art and senior high English.

I hadn't planned to be a teacher; it was something that happened while I wasn't looking. I hadn't planned to be a writer either. Writing is just something I've always done — for myself — because it feels right. Getting my first book published was a happy accident, one that changed the entire focus of my life. Now I'm doing what I love to do every single day — and I couldn't be more thrilled